To Suzanne

Thank you –
for giving it a go.
I hope you like it!
Very first signing of the
very first copy!

RED MERCURY

Rod Gillies

ISBN-10: 1478223243
ISBN-13: 978-1478223245

For everyone who likes a bit of clank

The pilot pulled the gas mask from its box and then over his head, hauling on the straps until the rubber seal pinched at the skin of his face. Probably too tight, he thought, but he didn't want to risk breathing in any of the air from outside. Not now, not as they approached the crater. Satisfied with the fit of his mask, he reached out and flicked a switch on the control panel, activating warning lights in the other compartments throughout the airship, signalling to his crewmates and their passenger to don their own protective equipment.

Alerted by the flashing lamp, the man crammed uncomfortably into the observation turret pulled his eyes from the viewfinder for a moment. As he slipped the canvas and rubber breathing apparatus over his head, his hands were shaking. The level of devastation below was like nothing he had ever seen before, terrifying and exciting in equal measure.

Mask secure, he returned his gaze to the ground, cranking the handle on the box camera at regular intervals. The force of the blast wave must have been incredible. Even from this altitude, the trees were flattened as far as he could see, strewn out in arcs across the blackened earth, their scorched trunks stripped of lesser branches.

The crater itself was enormous, perhaps five hundred yards across, an almost perfect bowl shape scooped from the frozen ground. Of the buildings that had stood here previously, nothing remained. The village of Tunguska and its inhabitants were gone, vaporised in the first instant of the explosion. The observer smiled to himself as he continued with his photography. The General would be pleased.

Part One

The sky over the shipyard was a bright cloudless blue, the winter sunlight glinting off the gentle waves beyond the breakwater. A pleasant change from the Lake District's usual weather. Anderson couldn't recall a single trip up here during the last year when it hadn't been pouring with rain.

A whole year, almost to the day, since the project had got the nod to proceed from the Admiralty. Twelve months of training the crew in Southampton, punctuated by regular rail journeys north to Barrow to check on the steel skeleton of the vessel as it slowly took shape.

"Lovely day for it, eh skipper?"

Anderson turned to see the squat frame of his chief engineer bustling along the quay towards him. "It certainly is Mr Dixon. A good omen I think."

"Here's hoping." The engineer lowered his voice. "I just pray she's watertight cap'n. Sunny skies won't mean much if she springs a leak."

The man was a born pessimist, thought Anderson, his glass not so much half-empty as broken. Still, that healthy paranoia meant the chief now knew every seam, valve and rivet of his new charge even better than the shipyard workers who had put her together. As Dixon put it, "Always assume the worst, that way you'll only ever be pleasantly surprised." Whilst the man's outlook was bleak in the extreme, Anderson knew there was no better engineer in the Royal Navy.

"Stow that chatter Chief. I don't want you spooking the

crew."

The engineer straightened his shoulders. "Aye aye cap'n. Chatter stowed." His mouth retained its downward cast though.

"Cheer up man. You've seen even more of her than I have. She'll do us proud."

Anderson looked up the slipway towards the open doors of the assembly shed. There, just visible in an interior darkened by the contrast with the low sun, he could make out the bow of his new command – Her Majesty's Submersible *Nautica,* the first submarine vessel to enter Imperial service.

For years the Royal Navy had concentrated on the building of dreadnoughts at the expense of all else. Until recently, most Admirals had expressed a dismissive attitude to submersibles. The whole idea of waging undersea warfare was considered "damned difficult and damned unsporting."

But concerns about naval fair play were of little import to the Germans who had spent ten years developing their submarine fleet. Britannia was supposed to rule the waves, and the Admiralty had grown uncomfortable that Germany was now the unchallenged master of the ocean's depths. This simply would not do, and so the Empire's cadre of naval engineers had quietly turned their attention to submersibles. *Nautica* was the result, a prototype vessel designed to sail further, faster, and deeper than any other submarine.

Anderson pulled at the chain of his fob watch and flicked the dented casing open to check its face. The timepiece was nearly twenty years old now and the intervals it could sustain between winding were becoming shorter. He supposed he really ought to consider a replacement but the watch had been a gift from his wife to mark his first commission and he was fond of its familiar heft.

He raised his hand and waved, signalling to the workers waiting at the top of the ramp. They swung their heavy sledgehammers and knocked out the last two support posts beneath the submarine's bow. With a harsh metallic screech, the cradle holding the submarine began its progress down the greased slipway towards the water. The thick links of rusted chain dragging behind were designed to stop her picking up too much momentum, but the submersible had still reached a fair speed as she slid past Anderson and Dixon.

The vessel's rounded bow struck the water with a sharp slap, sending a wave surging out into the calm of the channel. *Nautica* slid forward, lowering herself into the water. Her front half disappeared beneath the surface for a moment before she bobbed slowly upward, finally free from the cradle which had held her since the first ribs of her keel had been laid.

Well at least she floats, thought Anderson, that's a start.

Dixon stepped to his Captain's side, his grin somewhat out of keeping with his usual demeanour. "Isn't she a beauty?"

"That she is Chief."

In truth, *Nautica* would never win any medals for her looks. She wallowed in the water as she was hauled in, an ungainly tube of wooden planking, riveted plates and hoops of steel. Sixty feet from bow to stern, and thirteen feet in diameter, her stubby cigar shape was broken only by the bulbous glass dome of her bridge and the steering fins mounted at her stern.

"Seems a shame not to have a band though", grumbled the engineer. "Don't seem proper without some kind of celebration."

Dixon was right. But no band, no ceremony, and above all, no reporters – that had been the decision. The Admiralty wanted the launch of *Nautica* to be kept as quiet as her construction. Ostensibly to prevent alerting the Germans to Imperial ambition beneath the waves, Anderson suspected the secrecy was also a way of avoiding any public embarrassment if the new vessel should prove less than watertight.

The gangway was run out from the quay and Anderson walked down its steep gradient, stepping out onto the hull of his new command for the first time. His officers and crew clambered aboard behind him, excited to see their boat finally afloat. Their short training dives to the bottom of the Solent in the navy's single bathysphere had whetted their appetites. To a man they were keen to get *Nautica* underwater, where she belonged.

"Right chaps," Anderson said to his assembled officers, "I want her fuelled, provisioned and ready to sail within the hour."

"Aye aye sir," they chorused before heading off in different directions, voices rising in shouted commands. The crewmen snapped into action, moving to their appointed tasks.

They were a good crew, thought Anderson as he walked forward to the access hatch. They should be. He had picked them himself, given a free hand by the Admiralty to select the best men in each specialty. He had also made sure they were all unmarried, or like himself, widowers without children. He figured that was probably for the best, especially in light of the orders he had received from London the previous evening.

*

The bitter cold seeping into Jones' extremities helped take his mind off the constant motion. It was a small blessing, but he'd take it. With the airship now side-on to the gusting wind, the gondola was swinging back and forth beneath the gasbag and his stomach rebelled with every lurch. Placing his hand out to steady himself, Jones felt the vibration through the metal plates of the hull as the engines strained to keep the craft on course. He was sure the airship was flying through winds well beyond what its manufacturers would have advised, but there wasn't much he could do about that. For the last three hours he'd done little more than peer out of the window into the night, trying to keep his supper down.

Jones was unused to feeling so powerless, and it filled him with frustration. It would have been a different matter had they been on a boat, whatever the weather. He'd been aboard many a race yacht pitched and tossed as badly, or worse, but had never felt so apprehensive. He was a strong swimmer, after all, but he couldn't fly.

He looked across the cockpit at the man in the pilot's chair, wondering if the airman would look quite so cheerful if the tables had been turned and they were out in the choppy Solent rather than in the wild skies high above Siberia. Wing Commander Wilberforce certainly appeared to be enjoying the flight, whooping and grinning with each plunge of the craft as he wrestled with the controls.

"Ha!" roared Wilberforce as the airship took another broadside gust. "This is my kind of flying. Better than a boring old jaunt over the Surrey countryside, eh?" He looked round and smiled at Jones. "How are you enjoying the flight Major?"

"Delightful, positively delightful," said Jones through gritted teeth. "Will the delightfulness be continuing for much longer?"

The airman's smile grew broader. "How the bloody hell should I know? I only point the thing where I'm told. Hold on a moment..." He reached for the speaking tube mounted to his left and flicked open the cover. "Navvy!" he bellowed. "How much longer? Our passengers are anxious to disembark."

Wilberforce drummed his fingers on the control column, waiting for a reply. "Burrows!" he shouted again. "Are you asleep back there? Have you got any bloody idea where we are?"

A voice crackled from the tube. "Yes sir. Right on course sir. Ten minutes to destination sir."

"Are you sure? You're not working from that blasted abacus thing again?"

"No sir. Double-checked by hand sir."

Wilberforce flicked the tube cover shut.

"There you go Major. The lad's too keen on that new-fangled Babbage thing, keeps wittering on about gyroscopes and magnetic tracking, but Burrows can plot a course. I'll grant him that."

Jones nodded and turned from the flight deck, heading

back down the narrow corridor, shoulders thumping the bulkhead first on one side and then on the other as the gondola swung. Ten more minutes and then we can throw ourselves into the night from a perfectly serviceable aircraft. Madness. He had seen quite enough of the insides of airships during the long journey from London to Aberdeen and then on to Finland, but that didn't mean he wanted to jump out of this one.

Three men were seated on the low benches in the rear compartment. Fitzgerald and Webster sat looking miserable, exhaling clouds of frozen breath, occasionally stamping one foot and then the other trying to keep their blood circulating. The third man, Kowalski, was fast asleep and snoring noisily, head leaning back on the metal fuselage, seemingly oblivious to the cold.

"Ten minutes, gentlemen" said Jones moving towards the packs piled up between the benches. "Time we were properly attired."

"Dressing for dinner, are we?" asked Webster as he pulled himself to his feet.

"Naturally. Did you expect anything less? Perhaps you could wake up our American cousin? We wouldn't want him to be late to the party now, would we?"

Kowalski came awake with a grunt as Webster shook his shoulder. He took a slow look round through gritty eyes and rolled his shoulders.

"Well Major," he said, "we finally getting out of this tin can of yours?"

"Not mine Captain, Her Majesty's."

"Heh. My apologies. We colonials ain't always the best at remembering the niceties."

"Don't worry about it. After all, the niceties are not why you are here."

Jones saw the look Kowalski gave him. The man wasn't stupid. Jones could almost read the question in his eyes: so why was he here? Jones would tell him soon enough. For now it was enough that Kowalski was the only one of them who'd ever dropped from an airship before.

The men shuffled around the compartment, pulling first the metal wing assemblies and then the bulky packs onto their shoulders. They took turns to check each other's buckles and straps, fastening them as tightly as they could.

All had knives and pistols strapped to their belts and Kowalski had a repeating carbine tied across the top of his pack. Alongside rations and cold weather gear, the packs were stuffed with sticks of dynamite, fuses and timers. Manufacturers' marks and identifying insignia had been carefully removed from every item of equipment that wasn't genuine Soviet issue.

"Everyone ready?" Jones asked.

"Ready to get killed maybe..." Never the cheeriest of fellows, Fitzgerald looked distinctly unhappy. "This is ridiculous Major. Webster and I spend our time behind desks. We've never done anything like this before." Behind him, Webster's round face looked similarly troubled as he nodded in agreement.

"If it's any consolation, neither have I," said Jones. "However, the Captain here has dropped dozens of times and lived to tell the tale."

Webster snorted. "Well bully for the Captain, but surely there are whole squadrons of dragoons specially trained for this sort of thing?"

"You know there are. But few who could be mobilised in time, and fewer still that speak Russian. You heard the Duke, we were the best he could muster. Now," Jones looked hard at his fellow Englishmen, "are we going to jump out of this bloody thing, or am I going to have to throw you out one after the other?"

Webster looked resigned. "Very well Major. Let's get it over and done with." He turned to stand with Kowalski before the large bulkhead door at the rear of the compartment.

Fitzgerald held Jones' stare for a moment before his shoulders slumped in defeat. "Alright Major, you win. But if I make it to the ground in one piece, I demand one of those fancy Turkish cigarettes of yours as a reward."

"Fitz, if we both make it down in one piece, you can have the whole damned case."

*

Three nights before, sitting in the Duke of Buckingham's office in Whitehall, Jones had harboured many of the same reservations as Fitzgerald and Webster.

Hanson, the Duke's advisor, had welcomed them as they filed into the high-ceilinged room. "Gentlemen, thank you for joining us at such short notice this evening. I do hope you were not overly inconvenienced."

Jones' summons had arrived, in the hands of a junior officer, as he was sitting down to dinner with his aging aunt and uncle at their home in Richmond. Whilst they kept an excellent table, their conversation was generally dreadful and he had jumped at the opportunity to escape. Many a time over the next few days he was to find himself wishing he had stayed in Richmond, supping the rather fine soup, but then you didn't volunteer for Buckingham's Special Operations Division if you wanted a quiet life.

Buckingham himself sat behind an antique desk before a wall dominated by an enormous oil painting. A Gainsborough, if Jones remembered correctly, but not a good one. The Duke got to his feet as the men entered and shuffled round the desk to greet them, leaning heavily on his ivory-handled cane.

"Let us begin," he said, his moustache bristling as he spat words like machine gun bullets. "You've got a man to collect. A rescue mission. With an added helping of demolition."

He introduced the gathered men to one another. "This is Fitzgerald, and this is Webster. Two specialists from my Russian section. This disreputable-looking chap is Major Jones, on secondment to me from the Queen's Guards."

Webster thrust his podgy hand out. "Delighted to make your acquaintance old chap," he said as he pumped Jones' arm up and down enthusiastically. "Heard a lot about you."

Fitzgerald said nothing, only inclining his head as he and Jones shared a short, firm handshake.

The Duke indicated his other guest with the tip of his cane. "And this colourful character is John Kowalski, from Florida. A Captain in the infamous Free Fleet, no less."

Webster and Fitzgerald stared at the man with undisguised curiosity, and he gave a casual fingertip salute in response, barely acknowledging their presence. Jones assumed you got used to curious looks when people discovered you were a mercenary. The Floridian's sharp-eyed gaze spent more time looking over Jones however. Not a challenge, rather an appraisal, the measured assessment of one professional by another.

As the men settled themselves, Buckingham pulled a photograph from a folio of documents and tossed it onto the large mahogany table. The sepia image showed a balding man, perhaps sixty years old, with thick round glasses and a goatee beard.

"Our man is here," said the Duke, tapping on an unrolled map of Russia. "Kovdor Mine. Just outside Murmansk. Middle of bloody nowhere."

"Who is he sir?" asked Fitzgerald.

"Scientist. Jewish chap. Alexei Eisenstein. You chaps have to get him and his daughter out of there."

"Won't the Russians have something to say about that?"

"Yes, I imagine they would. If they knew anything about it. Which cannot happen. Small team of men. In and out before the comrades realise."

Hanson spoke up. "Stealth and discretion are essential. If it became apparent to the Soviets that Imperial agents were blundering around inside Russia then I daresay Lenin and his chums would be less than impressed."

Buckingham leaned over the table. "Germany and France seem set upon a collision course. Damned idiots. If that happens, we shall have no option but to honour our treaties and support the French. Now, we could have counted on Tsar Nicholas. But since those bloody Bolsheviks took over?" The Duke harrumphed into his moustache. "The whole thing is up in the air. The Soviets might make for uncomfortable allies, what with all that socialism claptrap, but we cannot afford to push them into the arms of the Kaiser."

Webster looked up from the map. "I can appreciate the

need for discretion, but why us? I mean, why Fitzgerald and I?" He indicated the other men round the table. "The Major I know, if only by reputation, and I'm sure Captain Kowalski is capable enough. But Fitzgerald and I are bureaucrats, bloody paper-shufflers, if you'll excuse my French. Granted, we did some sneaking around when we were young, but that was nearly ten years ago." He patted at the paunch barely contained within his waistcoat. "I can hardly climb the stairs without getting out of breath nowadays, never mind a rope, or God forbid, a wall."

Buckingham raised his cane, waving it in Webster's direction. "I don't see you with one of these yet. You'll manage."

Hanson stepped forward. "Local knowledge could turn out to be the key to this mission. Granted it is some time since either of you were out in the field, but I doubt there is an Englishmen alive who has spent as much time in northern Russia as you two."

Webster and Fitzgerald glanced at one another, clearly unhappy.

"Chin up chaps," said Buckingham. "You'll have Major Jones leading your little excursion. What you may lack in recent field experience, he makes up for in droves. And we're lucky enough that the Captain here was available at short notice. I'm sure he can be guaranteed to supply any required, ah, muscle." The Duke jabbed his cane at Kowalski. "That's the word you colonials use, I believe?"

"Something like that, Your Lordship."

"We are short on time, and short on people. Hence retaining the services of Captain Kowalski, as well as pulling you men in with such little notice."

"Interrupted a damned good dinner doing it too," said Jones.

The Duke turned towards him, eyebrow arched. "I thought you were awfully quiet Major. I assume you have some questions."

Jones slipped his hand into his jacket and took out his cigarette case. He opened it and removed one of the slim, white cylinders, rolling it backwards and forwards between his thumb and forefinger. Eventually he looked up at the Duke. "Only the obvious one. This Eisenstein chap, what's he working on?"

"Now Major," said Hanson, "let's just say there are certain details you don't need to be acquainted with in order to carry out your duties."

"My experience in the field is regularly to the contrary." Jones lit his cigarette and blew out a cloud of fragrant smoke. "I find being in full possession of the facts often makes it easier to get the job done."

"As I said, things you do not need to know. Now moving on –"

"I just wondered, if it might have something to do with Red Mercury?"

Hanson's eyes narrowed. "How could you possibly know that?"

"Well, let's say I happen to know Murmansk is one of the few places in the world where uranium ore is concentrated in quantities where it can be effectively mined. And you've already told us we're going to infiltrate a mine. And let's say I also happen to know uranium is a key ingredient in this Red Mercury stuff which everyone seems to be excited about."

Jones took another draw on his cigarette before continuing. "As to how I know these things? Let's say there are certain details you don't need to be acquainted with in order to carry out *your* duties, Mr Hanson."

"That's quite enough." The Duke cut in to prevent the exchange continuing. "Hanson, I think these men have heard enough to make further secretiveness pointless. Tell them."

Hanson looked fit to burst, but began to speak. "The Kovdor mine is being used to extract and purify uranium ore for conversion into Red Mercury. Current methods are painfully slow. In five years, the mine has produced no more than four ounces of the stuff. Our man Eisenstein is perfecting a new process that will allow them to do things much more efficiently." He tapped his finger on the photograph of the scientist. "The Professor contacted us a week ago, through channels you *definitely* do not need to be acquainted with. He wants out."

"Why? And why now?" asked Jones.

"Eisenstein is no Bolshevik. His wife was held in a labour camp to ensure his loyalty, but she died last month. His daughter works with him at the mine, and he will not leave Russia without her. The longer we leave it, the more likely the Soviets will move her somewhere else as they did with his wife. Leverage, you see."

The Duke spoke up once again. "The head man in Murmansk is no fool. Met him once, at a summit in Warsaw. General Gorev – great brute of a chap. Handshake like a vice. Very bright though. Ambitious too."

"He's done very well for himself since the Revolution," said Hanson. "Runs their Committee of Scientific

Advancement. Favourite of Lenin's apparently."

Jones ground his cigarette into the ashtray. "From what I hear, Comrade Lenin's favour can wax and wane somewhat. Just ask Trotsky. How are we to get into Russia?"

Kowalski raised his hand. "Whoa there. Slow up a little. There are still a bunch of things I need to get straight. What does this here Red Mercury stuff do?"

Hanson hesitated, glancing at the Duke who nodded for him to continue. "Red Mercury is a deadly poison, but one that does not need to be touched or inhaled. It can sicken and kill from a distance. Beyond these immediate unsavoury properties, if prepared correctly it can be used to make bombs which explode with astonishing force."

"Like nitro-glycerine then, but poisonous?"

Hanson shook his head. "Red Mercury makes Mister Nobel's concoction look positively harmless. A one-pound bomb could destroy the entire city of London and poison its ruins for a hundred years."

Silence descended as the assembled men pondered this information.

Eventually the Duke spoke. "The four ounces that Hanson mentioned? The Bolshies used it in a test two months ago. Blew a bloody great hole in Siberia. They've got the know-how, and now they're on the verge of being able to produce Red Mercury in quantity." He shook his head. "If the Soviets build more of these bombs, a conflict between France and Germany will be immaterial, a petty little disagreement. With such a weapon, Communist Russia would sweep across Europe and Great Britain unchallenged, and I doubt even your United States could stand against her Captain."

"Not my United States, Your Lordship. I'm Floridian. But I get the gist of it."

"We simply have to get Eisenstein and his daughter out. And put a serious dent in the operation of that damned mine." He looked at each man in turn. "Now, this is obviously a mission for volunteers. You're all free to leave now if you wish. Time to decide chaps. In or out?"

Jones nodded. "Whilst I reckon they'd struggle to get an airship close, I don't fancy the thought of the Bolshies sneaking a bomb up the Thames on some tatty old steamer. I'm in."

Webster and Fitzgerald looked at each other uncomfortably for a moment before they too nodded their agreement.

Kowalski shrugged. "I go where the Fleet tells me, Your Lordship. Just so long as you keep paying the bills."

"Very well gentlemen," said Hanson. "If you could all come with me, we have a railway special waiting at Victoria. You're off to the aerodrome at Farnborough. First stop, Aberdeen. We'll finish briefing you up there."

The Duke shook their hands and wished them luck as they filed out, but he placed his hand on Jones' shoulder as he brought up the rear. "Hang on a moment Major. I need a word."

Buckingham let the others continue after Hanson down the corridor. He closed the door and turned to Jones. "Sorry David, but I haven't been totally honest with you. Things are not as simple as they may appear..."

*

"Five minutes to destination!" crackled Wilberforce's

voice through the speaking tube.

"Right chaps. Let's get ready," said Jones.

Kowalski stood at the door, watching the three Englishmen as they shuffled into line. Webster looked terrified, Fitzgerald angry. Jones was impassive as ever. Kowalski wondered if the man ever got flustered.

"Gentlemen," he said. "When it's your turn to drop, you will take a large step forward over the threshold with your arms crossed over your chest. Clear?"

The men nodded. He had talked them through the drop procedure umpteen times in the last few days until they could all repeat his lines without even thinking. But this time it was no drill.

"You will count to ten. No more. No less. Then you will pull the cord and your wings will deploy. If your wings fail to deploy, do not panic. Reach around to the small of your back and pull the rope handle you will find at the base of the assembly. Can you all feel the rope handle now?"

The men all checked and nodded once more.

"Follow the wing-lamps of the man ahead of you, adjusting your body position like we practiced. Make sure you ain't bunching up on the man ahead, or falling too far behind."

He resisted the urge to smile as he recalled the 'practice' he had taken them through over the last few days in spartan military accommodations, first in northern Scotland and then Finland. The three Englishmen, lying on their stomachs across mess room chairs, attempting to keep their arms and legs stretched out, rocking backwards or forwards as he had shouted directions. He had made no attempt to teach them how to make the mental calculations from their altitude and descent speed gauges, coming up with the much simpler plan of them following him and watching his wing lamps.

"As we approach the ground, I'll activate my props. My wing-lamps will change to red automatically. When you see the lamps of the man ahead of you change, count to five and then activate your own props by throwing the chest lever."

The men's hands all moved up to find the metal lever protruding from the chest box on their harness.

"Count to ten, pull the cord. Red light, count to five and throw the lever. That's all you need to remember. After that, it's a piece of cake."

Aerial dragoons trained for months before they had their first drop. Kowalski had done his best to get these men ready in a fraction of that time. He hoped it was adequate preparation for a night drop through unfriendly skies. He figured he'd done what he'd been paid for. The rest was up to them.

*

Burrows entered the compartment and pointed past the assembled men who parted to let him through. The navigator clipped his safety line to a wall bracket and grasped the wheel on the bulkhead door.

"Ready?"

"As we'll ever be, Mr Burrows," answered Jones for them all.

Wilberforce's voice echoed out once again. "Approaching destination. Open the hatch."

The airman turned the wheel and began pulling the door inwards. The wind hurled itself through the widening gap, dropping the temperature in the compartment even further. Kowalski pulled his leather facemask down and adjusted the fit of the goggles. Jones and the others did the same. Preparation over, they waited amidst the noise and cold, trying to avoid thinking about what was to come.

"Ready to drop..." came the voice from the tube. As Wilberforce's amplified tones crackled their way through the countdown, Burrows held up his hand, displaying the numbers with his fingers before Kowalski's face.

"Five..." Kowalski shuffled forwards to the edge of the door.

"Four..." He tugged one last time on the straps of his harness.

"Three..." He crossed his arms over his chest, Burrows keeping him steady in the doorway with a firm grip on his shoulder.

"Two..." He took a last glance back and nodded to the men behind him.

"One!" Without a pause Kowalski stepped forward and tipped headfirst into the darkness.

Webster hesitated only a moment and followed, although less gracefully than Kowalski. Fitzgerald stood unmoving. Burrows grabbed the reluctant man's shoulder, hauling him forward.

Jones shoved sharply from behind. "Get out of that bloody door Fitz!"

Fitzgerald turned, eyes wide behind his goggles. Jones prepared himself to push the man through the opening, but seeing the intent, Fitzgerald turned back, grabbed the sides of the hatch and threw himself out into the night unaided.

Jones paused for a moment himself, still astonished he

was really going to go through with this. He was roused by Burrows thrusting a small, oilskin-wrapped package into his hand. Jones looked at it stupidly and then stuffed it into a pocket of his snow suit jacket. He nodded his thanks to the other man and stepped forward out of the door.

He tumbled in the air, catching a vague glimpse of the airship's bulk before it disappeared in the darkness. The fierce blast of the wind forced its way through the fabric of his clothing and facemask, producing a chill like ice splinters where it found skin. Jones tried to concentrate on his count, distracted by his racing heartbeat as he plummeted through the night. Reaching ten, he pushed his arm down against the rush of air, hunting for the flailing release cord. The cable slipped from his grasp at first, causing him a moment of sick panic, but on his second attempt, he grabbed hold and pulled. With a sudden jerk, the wings deployed from the assembly on his back, and he felt a flood of relief course through him as his rate of descent began to slow.

Definitely slower, but still fast enough to break every bone in his body when he hit the ground. Craning his head to the side, he checked his props. There, barely visible in the darkness, the prop blades mounted halfway down the metal wings were spinning furiously, exactly as they were designed to do. The props would build up pressure in his chest box as he fell, pressure which would be converted into motive power when he threw the lever, reversing the direction of the props' rotation, creating lift and slowing his descent.

The theory was simple, and in practice it came down to one key element – throwing the lever at the right moment.

Too soon and you would not have built up enough pressure, causing gravity to rudely reassert itself before you were safely down. Too late and you would have plenty of pressure but not enough time to slow before you smashed headlong into the ground. As Kowalski had wryly informed them, falling had never hurt anybody. Abrupt deceleration was what you had to worry about.

Jones began searching the sky below for his fellows and soon spotted a pair of green lights beneath him and off to the left – Fitzgerald. After a moment he made out another two lights further down, to the right this time – Webster. Finally, far beneath him, leading the descent, the final pair – Kowalski. Thank God the night was clear, otherwise they would never have been able to spot one another. But there they all were, wings safely deployed.

He watched as Webster's lights began drifting right, bringing him into line with Kowalski. Fitzgerald was moving too, but with more seesawing, overcompensating first one way and then the other. Jones rolled his shoulders a little, and watched the lights below him shift. He straightened up and moved back a touch, finding the right balance between the forward momentum given him by his wings and the strong wind. Surprised at how stable he felt, Jones was shocked to realise he was almost enjoying the sensation. He wondered how it would feel to try this in daylight, to see the panorama of the earth spread out below. And maybe somewhere warmer he thought, the biting slipstream continuing to stab its way through his multiple layers.

Below him the lowest set of lights changed to red. Jones began counting to himself and, sure enough, on five,

Webster's wing-lamps changed colour. Another five and Fitzgerald's also turned crimson.

After making his own count, Jones grabbed the lever on the chest box and threw it. With a screech of shifting gears, his props began their counter-rotation and his harness jerked tighter, driving the breath from his lungs.

They flew in closer formation now and Jones could make out shadowy shapes of wings and men in the glow of the thin crescent moon. In the same faint, silvery light he began taking note of the surroundings, rather than simply concentrating on the lamps of the men below. They were falling, more and more slowly as their props spun, towards a snow-covered waste dotted with patches of darker forest. Away to the north, perhaps ten miles or so, a faint cluster of lights could only be Murmansk.

Kowalski's wing-lamps began slipping to the left and the three Englishmen followed with varying degrees of grace. The Floridian was leading them towards a field near one of the small clusters of trees. Jones hoped the snow was deep, and soft.

The last few moments were a blur. Although rationally he knew his rate of descent had reduced dramatically, the white ground still appeared to be approaching at a terrifying rush. Remembering Kowalski's training, he lifted his head and arms to swing his body almost vertical. He pushed his legs out before him, feet together. Nothing he could do now but brace for the impact.

Jones thumped hard into the snow, his landing burying him deep in the drift. Lying there, staring up at the dark sky above, he wiggled his fingers and toes in turn, then gingerly moved his arms and legs. He was astonished to find himself whole and undamaged. He pulled the mask and goggles from his face and let out a long relieved breath.

Unclipping his harness, Jones struggled to his feet. He detached the wing assembly and chest box from the rest of his pack and tossed them aside. He withdrew an electrical lamp from the pack and flashed it briefly to each of the four points of the compass.

First to lumber out of the snow towards his signal was Webster, almost breathless with excitement. "Quite astonishing, eh Major?" he panted, face flushed and eyes gleaming. "Once I realised I was unlikely to die, I found that most invigorating."

"Here's hoping Fitz felt the same, I practically had to push him out the door."

"Poor dear. I did think the old boy was looking a little green around the gills."

They both turned as Kowalski and Fitzgerald trudged out of the darkness together.

"Everybody alright?" asked the Floridian.

"Quite well Captain," chirped Webster. "Keen to have another go, actually."

"I told you you'd get the hang of it."

Fitzgerald looked sourly at the rest of them. "I swear, if I ever have to do something like that again, I'll kill myself first."

"Cheer up Fitz," said Jones, "Let's get into the trees for a bit of cover. And then you can have that smoke I owe you."

The other man perked up at this. "Ah yes. I believe you owe me the whole case."

"Don't push your luck. I nearly had to throw you out of

the damn thing up there."

"You did indeed, Major. Let's call it quits with the one."

The four men gathered their gear and headed towards the trees.

*

They moved north through the snow-covered countryside, staying inside the cover provided by patches of woodland wherever possible. Whilst the uneven ground between the pines made for difficult going, none of them complained. Although it was hard work concentrating on their footing between the trees, it was infinitely preferable to the apprehension they all felt in the pit of the stomach when forced to cross any larger patches of open ground. Regardless of their fears, they encountered no signs of life. The entire land around them seemed frozen solid in a deep winter sleep.

Hours passed during which the sky brightened as much as it would at this time of year. The pale sun limped up over the horizon, bringing a little light but no warmth. Despite the bitter chill in the air, Jones found himself sweating profusely, his thighs burning with the effort of dragging his legs through the knee-high snow. At least the terrain they traversed was reasonably flat. He wasn't sure they would have managed if there had been any hills to contend with.

They had taken turns leading the way, the first man in line forging a path for the others, but it was exhausting work out in front and he and Kowalski had taken the lion's share of leading as the other two struggled. Stopping at regular intervals in the scattered patches of forest to recover their strength, the four men had made torturous progress through the morning. But it couldn't be far now, Jones thought, his eyes fixed on the next line of trees.

Moving into cover past the first few trunks, he slipped his pack from his shoulders and sank to the ground, leaning back against a dark, moss-covered pine. Fitzgerald and Webster shuffled up and collapsed in ungainly fashion, both of them wheezing badly.

"Good Lord," groaned Webster, "I'm in worse bloody shape than I thought. I sound like a set of broken bagpipes. I have got to do something about this midriff of mine." He slipped his backpack from his shoulders and flopped back full length into the snow. "Mind you, at least my extra layer helps me keep warm. I don't know how a gangly rake like you can stand it Fitz."

"Don't you worry about me old boy. All I need is a smoke every now and again. Nothing like it for warding off the chill." He cast a dark look towards Jones. "Although goodness knows when we'll be allowed another one..."

"Funny," said Webster, "never developed a taste for tobacco myself. Plenty of other vices of course..."

"Talking of smoke, I can see some rising above the trees ahead," said Kowalski, still on his feet, relatively fresh from his stint at the rear of the line.

"Murmansk I hope," replied Jones, "unless we are quite spectacularly lost and have arrived somewhere else."

"Major, there ain't anyplace else to arrive *at*."

"Well we'd best go and take a look, just to be sure." Jones got to his feet. "Fitz, Webster – you two stay here with the equipment. Get some food inside yourselves. No fire, no noise, and sorry Fitz, still no smoke. The Captain and I shall head forward to get the lie of the land."

The men on the ground nodded, clearly relieved at the

prospect of a decent rest. Jones and Kowalski left them and pressed on. Without discussion, the two men began moving carefully, checking their footing with every step, slipping silently through the woods. One would head forward then pause, pressed against a tree, whilst the other moved past him. It was a pleasure to work with a fellow professional, reflected Jones, as he considered the natural pattern he and Kowalski had fallen into.

At the edge of the trees, they dropped to the ground, crawling the last few feet. From a vantage point under the firs they looked out over the bleak approaches to Murmansk. The wood at their backs stood on a small rise above a rough track of frozen, rutted mud. The track ran about half a mile to their left before disappearing between more trees. Half a mile in the opposite direction, it curved round to the north to meet the end of a metal-framed bridge crossing the steely grey river. Two guards stood at the end of the bridge, hands tucked into their armpits, trying to keep warm.

Across the river, the town squatted: a dismal collection of ramshackle sheds, dilapidated warehouses and ugly brick factories with towering chimneys. Tattered red flags snapped in the chill wind and plumes of steam billowed from vents and grilles, mixing with clouds of smoke to form a grim smog. Where the river met the waters of the Kola Sound, cargo ships moored at the dockside beneath a forest of cranes.

With a mechanical groan and a great hiss of steam, a tractor dragging a heavily-laden sledge emerged from one of the riverfront warehouses directly opposite them, grinding its way along the road towards the docks. The two observers spotted men in greatcoats and furred hats, somehow insignificant against the leaden backdrop of grey buildings. The tiny figures trudged the streets, hunched up against the cold, trailing little puffs of frozen breath as if they too were steam-driven.

"Welcome to the workers' paradise..." said Jones.

"Honestly Major, it don't seem much different from the less salubrious parts of London I've seen. Or New York, for that matter."

"Careful now Captain. You're beginning to sound like a Bolshevik."

"Heh. No danger of that. I'm all for free enterprise. And I can't abide the vodka the Reds all drink. I'm a bourbon man through and through." He stiffened, head to one side, listening. "What's that?"

Jones heard it too, and then felt the vibration in the ground beneath him. "We're about to have company."

Off to their left came the rumbling of heavy machinery over a slow rhythmic thump. The sound grew louder as its source approached, coming into view where the path emerged from the trees. Striding down the track, its two massive steel feet crunching through the frozen mud, a mechanical walker led a column of soldiers.

The walker's metal bulk towered over the men marching behind. Its body was a steel cube, ten feet square and studded with rivets and grilles, the forward panel dominated by a short, fat cannon barrel, like some kind of ugly snout. Above the gun, a slatted viewport allowed the pilot within to see where he was headed. Gears turned and the pistons mounted on the walker's legs expanded and contracted with sharp squeals of steam, propelling the vehicle forward in an unstoppable gait.

As they watched the walker lurch along the track, Jones dreaded to think how it would feel to be shaken back and forth inside the two-legged behemoth. Mind you, it would be a sight warmer in there than it was for the soldiers marching behind.

The company was made up of a hundred men or so, lined up in ranks of four. Although their boots and greatcoats were filthy and their marching was out of step over the broken track, the men held their heads high and carried their weapons with assurance. These were no raw conscripts, they looked like capable veterans.

"Major," whispered Kowalski, "that's a lot of soldiers. And they're all heading in the same direction as us."

"Hardly surprising. Murmansk is a barracks town for the Red Army."

"And we're going to stroll right on in there?" Kowalski looked aghast.

"Every week hundreds of soldiers arrive and depart by land, air and sea. With so many comings and goings, who is likely to notice four strangers? It's perfect."

"Major, you have a damned funny definition of perfection. I reckon the Fleet should have charged that Duke of yours something extra for all this..."

They lay in silence as the line of troops filed past, the dull thump of the walker's heavy feet turning to harsh metallic clangs as the column moved onto the bridge. When the last rank of marching men had moved past the observers' position, Jones and Kowalski shuffled back into the trees.

*

The men moved west through the woods, seeking an unobtrusive point where they could join the track. After half an hour's careful, quiet walking, they found the perfect spot where the trees stood right alongside the rutted road.

The party shrugged out of their snowsuits revealing Red Army uniforms beneath. Jones had the shoulder boards and decorations of a Major, Kowalski a Captain, and Webster and Fitzgerald both wore the rank of Sergeant. Greatcoats were pulled from packs and fur hats with red star insignia completed the outfits. However, as they finished changing, Jones realised something was still missing.

"Mud," he said. "We need some mud. Those soldiers we saw were filthy. I don't want to end up in some gulag because of a pristine greatcoat."

Fitzgerald stamped his foot on the hard ground. "We'll have to soften this up, and I don't think a fire is a good idea."

"Definitely not a good idea, but perhaps the comrades may have helped us with their little parade earlier..."

Jones checked the road was empty in both directions and stepped out from the woods. Sure enough, within a few yards he found what he was looking for. There, where the walker's steps had cracked through the surface ice, lay a dark patch of dirty water, not quite refrozen. He waved the others out and they took turns to stamp through the filthy liquid, spattering their coats with mud. Within a minute or two their uniforms looked more lived-in, if not quite as bedraggled as the soldiers they had seen earlier.

"Right then gentlemen. On into Murmansk. Follow my lead, and Russian only from now on."

As they trudged up the riverside track toward the bridge,

the two guards watched them approach. They seemed neither suspicious nor particularly alert, but Jones saw Kowalski adjust his grip on the carbine all the same.

"Relax Captain," he muttered, "New faces all the time, remember."

Approaching the guards, he pulled a cigarette from his case and held it up, calling out in fluent Russian. "Comrade Corporal, do you have a match? Or even better, perhaps any vodka?"

The corporal smiled and pulled off one of his gloves in order to fish a squashed box of matches from his pocket. "No vodka unfortunately, Comrade Major, but at least I can supply with you a light."

"Thank you," said Jones, taking the proffered box, striking a match and lighting his cigarette from cupped hands. "I am to report to the Comrade General when I arrive. Where would I find him?"

"The General spends most of his time out at the mine. This time of year, the only way out there is the train. The next one isn't until tomorrow morning."

"Very well. And the Cheka office? I need to speak to someone there."

A flicker of distaste crossed the soldier's face, but the emotion was quickly hidden. Nobody wanted to fall foul of the Soviet secret police. He turned and pointed over the bridge. "Straight up the road Major. Keep going until you reach the square."

"Thank you again Comrade. For the light, and for the directions. Shame about the vodka though..." Jones gave the guard a salute and marched onward.

The others followed him onto the bridge. Gaps between

its plating offered glimpses of the turbulent brown water below, dotted with chunks of ice churning their way downstream. The river was the reason for Murmansk's existence: its fast flowing current kept the Kola Sound free of sea ice, even in the depths of the Siberian winter, making the town the primary supply port for the whole of northern Russia.

Safely out of earshot of the guards, Kowalski spoke. "Nice work Major."

"Thank you Captain, although I fear our charades are only just beginning."

Over the bridge they entered the town, the road now hemmed in by the high brick walls of factories and warehouses. The buildings were arranged in haphazard fashion, tight alleyways cutting between them at odd angles. Founded only ten years previously, Murmansk was clearly the result of a rush of unplanned construction.

Through every doorway and dirty window pane they could see signs of military preparation. In workshop after workshop, men scuttled around, lit by the dull glow of forges and the sharp spray of sparks, feeding voracious machines with coal and steel. Inside one building they spied a half-assembled walker standing tall, still awaiting the attachment of its armoured plating. In another, they saw great bundles of rifles and stacks of shells. The town was filled with the sights and sounds of fearsome industry.

"Our friend Ivan is getting ready for war," muttered Fitzgerald.

"It's the same all across Europe," replied Jones, leaning close to the other man. "The difference is we all know who we're going to be fighting. Ivan hasn't decided yet."

The road up from the riverfront was full of workers and men in uniform, stomping here and there, nobody dawdling in the cold. The infiltrators were forced to stand aside along with everyone else to let large steam tractors rumble past, their massive wheels standing taller than a man. Amongst all the hurly-burly, nobody paid the four of them the least notice, except for the odd salute directed at Jones whenever a soldier spotted his collar pips.

As they approached the centre of the town, a group of men in patched and filthy coats shuffled down the muddy street, their steps hampered by the shackles connecting each man to his neighbour. Painfully thin, with shaved heads and sunken eyes, they looked like a battalion of the walking dead.

Jones grabbed the arm of a passing soldier and indicated the wretched parade. "Who are they?"

"Who knows? Poor bastards did something to upset the Cheka, and next thing they know, they're doing shifts as diggers out at the mine." The man shook his head and moved on.

They watched as the pitiful band filed past, perhaps thirty in all. At their rear marched a Russian sergeant, shouting and aiming the occasional kick at the prisoners to keep them moving. Jones would have dearly loved to give the overseer a kick of his own, and glancing at Kowalski he saw his own anger reflected in the Floridian's dark gaze.

"Now is not the time, Comrade Captain," he said, turning and leading the others up the road.

As they crossed the bustling main square a dark shadow overtook them, the throbbing of engines drifting down from above. Murmansk's residents were used to the sight of airships, but even so, soldiers and workers stopped in the street to stare and point at the dark grey bulk of a huge dirigible as it moved over the town, its ribbed gas envelope blocking out the sun. At an altitude of only a hundred feet or so, it flew low enough that those on the ground could make out figures at the bridge windows and the stubby cannon barrels poking out at all angles from the gunports down its sides.

One of the really big ones, a Tupolev surely, thought Jones, almost as big as the German Zeppelins. Heading for the air marshalling yards to the north of the town, no doubt. From there the Soviet airship fleet ranged out, supplying and protecting the isolated mining and drilling operations scattered across the islands of the Arctic. He knew people back in Whitehall were concerned at the growing capability of Soviet aeronautic forces – one reason everyone worried which way Russia would turn in the event of war. If it wasn't the German navy, it was Soviet airships – the days of unrivalled Imperial power seemed to be at an end.

As the enormous airship droned on, movement across the square resumed, pedestrians once again dropping their heads against the wind and trudging on. Jones and his men crossed the open space, dodging between horse-drawn sledges and noisy tractors, heading for a narrow street on the opposite side.

At the corner of the square, their way into the alley was blocked by a group of uniformed men, gathered around a commotion. Two men clad in black leather trenchcoats kicked at a young soldier curled into a ball on the ground, his hands held up around in his head in a feeble attempt at protection. The spectators looked on in sullen silence, wincing in sympathy as the blows rained in on their unfortunate comrade. One or two muttered their displeasure at the scene, but none dared intervene.

The grizzled old soldier in front of Jones turned away, unable to watch as another kick thumped into the helpless man. His eyes shone with tears but lit up with sudden hope when he spotted Jones' insignia.

"Comrade Major, you have to help." He clutched at Jones' sleeve. "My brother's son. He did nothing wrong. He was just lucky at the card table. Now these pigs are sober, they want their money back. Please..."

Other soldiers around them grumbled their agreement, looking to the senior officer now in their midst to take action. Damn it, thought Jones. The last thing they needed now was to draw attention, but as the older man's voice grew more desperate, Jones found himself at the centre of an expanding circle of expectant stares. He would have to do something. Walking away now would be as bad as intervening. He shoved his way past the pleading man and strode up to the policemen and their victim.

"That's enough Comrades," he said.

The two Chekists turned, their anger at the interruption fading to a dull simmer of resentment as they took in Jones' rank.

"This man was interfering with the work of the Cheka – " said one.

"As am I," snapped Jones. "Will I receive similar treatment? Whatever work you were about, it is finished."

He glared at the two men and they slowly backed away. The old soldier rushed forward and helped the injured man climb unsteadily to his feet.

“What is going on here?” rose a voice from the edge of the crowd.

The onlookers parted to reveal a tall figure, it too clad in the trademark dark coat of the Cheka, but leant an even more sinister aspect by the black patch over his left eye. A livid scar emerged from beneath the patch and ran down his cheek, pulling the corner of his mouth up in a cruel half-smile.

The two policemen snapped to attention as the newcomer stepped into the circle of soldiers. He turned his head, his single eye fixing on each man as if filing the face away for later identification. None of the assembly met his gaze, instead developing a sudden interest in the hard-packed snow beneath their feet. Soldiers on the fringes of the crowd began slinking away as unobtrusively as they could.

The man settled his attention on Jones. “Is there a problem Major?”

“A small discussion. A trivial matter. Nothing to concern yourself with.”

“A trivial matter, eh? Such a throng gathered for a mere discussion?” The man turned, staring expectantly at his men. “Well?”

The two policemen shared a look before they spoke. “The Major is correct...” said the first.

“... It was nothing. A misunderstanding,” finished the other.

They shifted uncomfortably under the one-eyed man’s stare but said nothing more.

The Cheka officer turned back to Jones. “Well Major, your trivial matter does indeed seem to be settled. For the moment." He raised his voice. "This gathering will disperse. Immediately."

As the surrounding soldiers began to move off, the man stepped up closer to Jones. "I will talk further with my men. Who knows? Perhaps you and I will end up having a small discussion of our own?"

"I look forward to it."

The uninjured side of the officer's face formed a brief, cold smile. He turned on his heel and marched off, his subordinates in tow.

Fitzgerald sidled up to Jones. "Excellent stuff Major. Perhaps you could have picked a more public place for your little performance?"

Much as Fitzgerald's tone needled him, Jones couldn't really disagree with the sentiment. "Probably not. Let's get moving before anything else happens."

As they entered the alley, they passed the old soldier tending to his beaten nephew, wiping at his bloodied face with a dirty rag. The veteran nodded gratefully at Jones before returning his attention to the younger man.

The four men proceeded up the road, dirty brick walls looming over them on either side. Jones counted road junctions and turned left at the appropriate corner, hoping the maps provided by Hanson's agents had been correct. Sure enough, a few hundred yards down the alley they came to a rail yard full of freight cars. The far side of the snow-covered space was taken up by an open-sided shed, a large black locomotive sheltering beneath its high roof, two passenger cars and a half-dozen coal trucks attached behind.

Across the yard from the engine shed, beyond the static

rolling stock, stood a dilapidated wooden hut, its low roof laden with snow, icicles hanging from the broken guttering. Gathering the men in the lee of one of the cars, Jones indicated the tatty building.

"Our accommodation, gentlemen," he said.

"One would normally turn one's nose up at such lodgings," said Webster. "But if it gets me out of the cold, it's as good as the bloody Ritz."

Kowalski nodded. "Amen to that."

"How can we be sure it's empty?" asked Fitzgerald.

"It's the old telegraph office. The Bolshies built another one in the centre of the town and Hanson's contacts swear this one is never used. But you're right, we cannot be sure. Someone will have to go and check. Captain Kowalski, if you would be so kind?"

"My pleasure, Major."

"Quietly, if you don't mind."

"Well obviously."

*

Climbing the steps onto the low wooden deck in front of the hut, Kowalski stepped carefully over to the padlocked door. Raising a gloved hand, he rubbed a clean patch on the filthy window pane and took a quick look inside. The hut appeared to be unoccupied.

He checked around, scanning the yard and the street beyond for any signs of movement. Confident he was unobserved, he drew his pistol. He also pulled a six-inch brass tube from the pocket of his greatcoat. This he screwed carefully onto the barrel of the gun.

The attachment was a new development from the Fleet's gunnery workshops. Whilst it ruined the balance of the weapon, and brought its effective range down to a matter of feet, it also dramatically reduced the noise of firing the pistol, making it almost silent. Just the thing for a secret mission he'd argued when Jones had raised concerns about taking along a piece of non-Soviet equipment. They had struck a compromise with Kowalski filing off the Floridian maker's mark.

He raised the pistol toward the padlock and fired. The noise of the shattered lock clattering to the planks was louder than the muffled pop of the shot itself. He gathered up the remains of the padlock, eased open the door and slipped inside.

The room held a wooden table and chairs and a small iron stove. One wall was taken up by a bureau desk covered in a jumble of wiring and telegraph gear. The layer of dust over the furniture implied the hut had been unused for some time. Kowalski checked the smaller room to the rear, confirming it too was empty. Lowering the blind over the window in there, and the one in the main room, he returned to the door, signalling to Jones and the others that all was clear.

"Nice little contraption you have there," said Webster when they were all inside. "We hardly heard the shot at all."

Kowalski held up the brass suppressor. "You English folks are mighty proud of your Imperial ingenuity, but us colonials have the odd trick or two up our sleeves."

"You certainly do Captain. Most impressive." Webster turned to Jones. "Well Major, what now?"

"Everyone needs to get some food and then some sleep. We're all dead on our feet, but at least now we've got a few hours in which to rest. In the morning the train will leave, and tomorrow it will be carrying an extra four passengers."

"And I suppose we'll be disguised as miners will we?" Fitzgerald shook his head. "It seems I neglected to pack my pickaxe Major."

"I'll work something out, Fitz. And I promise to let you know when I do."

Fitzgerald glowered, but said no more.

They risked lighting the small stove, figuring any wisps of smoke from the hut's chimney would be invisible against the general smog of Murmansk. Webster got a brew on and handed round mugs of scalding tea. Kowalski took a sip and grimaced, silently wishing they had brought some coffee along. The Brits and their damned tea. He moved as close to the stove as he could without catching fire.

He sighed in pleasure. "Now that is exactly what Momma Kowalski's little boy needed."

"Missing your Florida sun, Captain?" asked Webster.

"Mister, you have no idea. Florida boys ain't built for the snow, even ones with a Russian mother. This is the first time I've felt warm since we left London. Hell, it might even be colder here than when we stopped over in Aberdeen."

They all laughed.

"Russian parents?" asked Fitzgerald. He pulled blankets from his pack and tossed them to the other men.

"Momma. My father's Polish. They headed west when some Duke or Prince or somesuch cleared them off their land. Went to England first, but then took the boat to the States and ended up down in Florida. They're still there to this day, enjoying the sun."

Webster arranged his bedding on the floor. "The sun? Now that feels like a distant memory. This Florida of yours sounds most agreeable."

"It is. Well, if you can avoid the flies and the alligators, that is. The coasts and the towns are all pretty gentrified nowadays, but the interior? It still ain't much more than swamp."

"Makes one wonder why your neighbours to the north spent so long trying to reclaim the territory."

"Well, they sure talked a lot. But in all honesty, they didn't try that hard, and certainly not after the Fleet started proving itself useful."

"Ah yes, the Americans paid for your little excursion into Cuba, didn't they?"

"Damned if I'd describe it so. But at least it was warm..."

In truth, Cuba had been a hot, steaming cesspit. And dangerous too. It had been his first mission after signing up with the Fleet, dropping into the jungle to snuff out the Cuban revolution. He'd seen plenty more jungles since, all over south America.

Despite all his travels, this had been his first trip across the Atlantic, and definitely his first anywhere in such luxurious style. But damned if acting as security for a trade delegation from Miami wasn't the single most boring assignment he had ever received. He'd just begun wishing for a little less afternoon tea and a little more excitement when the telegram had arrived, instructing him to report to Whitehall.

Jones finished his tea and stood, interrupting Kowalski's thoughts.

“It’ll be getting dark soon. You three get some sleep. I’ll take the first watch.”

Kowalski lay down beside the others, shuffling as close to the stove as he dared. “What about you?” he asked once he was settled. “Or don’t you officer types need sleep?”

“I have always believed I’ll get more than enough sleep when I’m dead.”

“Heh. Careful what you wish for Major.”

Kowalski rolled over, pulling his blanket up around his chin.

*

Jones waited until the breathing of the three men on the floor fell into regular patterns. When he was sure they were all asleep he pulled a wooden box from his pack and crept over to the cluttered desk.

He gently tugged at the cable running down the wall, the rusty nails securing it coming free easily from the damp wood. Using the knife from his belt, he cut the cable and pared the covering off the ends, revealing the metal beneath. These bare wires he twisted around screws protruding from the rear of the box. He spun the wing nuts, securing the connections before he turned the unit the right way up.

The top of the unit was taken up by a metal plate and the spring-loaded hammer switch of a telegraph transmitter. Running along the front face, above a collection of brass switches and dials, was a line of wheels, like a stack of coins viewed side-on. Around the edges of the wheels were stamped small letters and numbers.

He glanced round to check the sleeping forms of his companions once more then flicked the rightmost of the unit's switches. There, at the limits of his hearing, he made out the faint clicking and whirring of the gears and rods inside the box as they began to turn and shift. Jones gave a sigh of relief. He had been worried the box's innards might have been damaged during the drop from the airship, but all seemed well.

Settling himself in his chair, he began turning the brass dials from one setting to the next. On his third adjustment the silver wheels along the front began to turn, displaying a row of letters. Got you, he thought, with a tight smile of satisfaction. He hunched over the telegraph, peering at the occasional message scrolling across the tumbler wheels, absorbing the information coming in and out of Murmansk. With the flick of one switch he could release the message to continue on its way. With another he could hold the telegram from its onward journey, or even reply to it himself.

As he read through the messages, he silently blessed the Imperial scientists beavering away at Bletchley Park, Buckingham's residence outside London. Jones had visited the workshops there and had come away both baffled and impressed by what he had seen. He wondered what the Russian and German High Commands would say if they knew British boffins were regularly intercepting telegraph traffic from across Europe and deciphering it using these automated machines.

After two hours checking on the intermittent messages, Jones was confident the Russians were still unaware of their presence. Or if they did know, they were keeping it awfully quiet. He straightened up to stretch his back and stifled a yawn. Time for a rest. Taking a bundle of old wiring from the heap on the desk, he placed it over the top of the newer equipment, concealing it from view. He moved over to the sleeping men and reached down to shake Kowalski awake. Jones waited for him to come to his senses before speaking.

"I've been thinking whilst you were asleep. I want to go into town and see if we can pick up any information."

"Risky, Major."

Jones gave a snort. "No more so than this whole bloody enterprise."

"Fair enough."

"Right. Two hours kip for me. Your turn on watch."

Kowalski glanced at the sleeping forms of the other men. Jones spotted the look.

"They haven't done this sort of thing for some time now Captain. I think we can leave them to their beauty sleep. After all, I'm sure the lovely maidens of Murmansk would agree those two need it more than we do."

"Heh. Undoubtedly Major, but if you've got any of those lovely maidens of yours hidden away somewhere, well I'd call it damned unsporting of you not to have shared."

Jones smiled as he arranged his blanket on the floor. "Sorry about that. But I didn't want to wake you, and the young lady in question had to rush off. The next one that happens along? You can have all to yourself."

"I'll hold you to that Major. My Momma would be delighted if I brought home a nice polite Russian girl."

"Well let's keep our eyes out for a suitable prospect, shall we? I should hate to disappoint the good Mrs Kowalski."

Jones lay his head down on his pack and gratefully

closed his eyes. He had long ago picked up the habit of grabbing snatches of rest whenever opportunities presented themselves, never sure when the next chance would arrive. He was asleep almost instantly.

*

Bleary-eyed from their all too brief rest, the men prepared to head out into the evening, stashing their equipment in the smaller room.

"I still don't see why we're taking this risk," complained Fitzgerald. "Especially after that nonsense in the square earlier. Or why we're going back out in the bloody cold before we absolutely have to."

"Firstly," said Jones, "I want to see if we can pick up any loose talk about the train, the mine, this chap Eisenstein, or even the blasted weather. Anything that might help us get the job done. Secondly, I don't know about you chaps, but I could do with a drink. And thirdly, and perhaps most importantly, I don't want to be stuck in here with you whining all evening Fitz."

Fitzgerald bristled. "Now hang on just a bloody minute Major. All I'm doing is trying to work out what the hell is going on. Not easy when you insist on playing your cards so close to your chest."

"Meaning what, exactly?"

"Meaning I think you have no idea how we're going to get aboard that train, and even if you had, you wouldn't tell us until morning. Would you?"

"Probably not," answered Jones, unwilling to reveal he had formed a plan whilst the others had slept. It wasn't necessarily a good plan, but it would do.

"Just as you have no intention of telling us how you'll

get us away from here in the unlikely event of us actually pulling this Professor out."

Jones' gaze grew hard. "Definitely not."

"Good God, but you're a cold bastard..."

"Maybe I am, but it keeps me alive, and I will not apologise to you for it." Jones stepped forward, his face only inches from Fitzgerald's. "You'll know exactly what I want you to know, exactly when I want you to know it, and not before. That way, if you're caught, you cannot tell the Bolshies a damned thing, no matter what they do to you."

Fitzgerald fell silent, cowed by Jones' harsh logic.

"You know how this works Fitz. I have to play it like this. There's a hell of a lot more than just our lives at stake here."

Fitzgerald slumped, his anger spent. "Very well Major, you win again. Let's go and get that drink. But you're bloody well buying."

"Done," nodded Jones, "but I am worried I seem to be spending my entire time bribing you with drinks and cigarettes..." He tried to make the comment a joke, but he was unable to keep the edge from his voice.

"I knew a girl like that in Cuba," said Kowalski in a wistful tone. All four men laughed, releasing the tension.

"Funny that," said Webster, "she sounds remarkably similar to one I knew in Berlin."

"Really? Do tell..." The Floridian put his arm around the shorter Englishman's shoulders as they moved outside into the freezing air. Quietly comparing notes, they led the way as the group made for the dim lights of the street beyond the ranks of freight cars.

*

Jones had found himself in some dubious hostelries in his time, but this basement dive was surely down there with the worst of them. The room was packed with a heaving mass of soldiers in varying states of inebriation, the cacophony from their shouting, laughter and singing filling the space under the low, bent ceiling beams. Faces everywhere were flushed from a combination of gutrot vodka and the stifling heat spewing from a huge iron stove in the corner. The floor was a sucking quagmire of inches-deep mud with only the odd plank here and there to provide more solid footing.

The combined smell of drunken sweat, stale beer and rough tobacco was enough to bring tears to the eyes. Jones' nose wrinkled further as he caught other odours suggesting that not all the patrons were bothering to stagger outside when they felt the call of nature.

There was no bar counter as such, simply a couple of wooden railway sleepers spanning the gap between two barrels. Behind this makeshift servery stood a burly barman in a filthy apron, his muscular arms crossed, surveying the crowd with a threatening scowl. Jones knew the type – poacher turned gamekeeper, fists itching for a sign of trouble, eager to get involved in a scrap.

When they had barged their way through the crowd, the barman had grunted in reply to their order, thumping down a bottle and four dirty glasses before scooping up Jones' coins with his meaty hand. As they turned from the bar, a nearby table of men had lurched to their feet and headed for the door. Jones and the others won the scramble for the vacant seats, and now huddled together in the cramped wooden booth.

The vodka was rough, but the peppery burn in the throat was almost welcome after the walk through the frozen streets. As they tipped the drinks back, Webster turned crimson and began coughing and spluttering, and Fitzgerald smothered a cough of his own. Kowalski smacked his empty glass back down on the table and sucked air over his teeth. "Comrade Major, you bring us to the nicest places."

"I aim to please, Comrade Captain."

Jones topped up all four glasses with the fierce liquid and then shoved the stopper back into the neck of the bottle. "That's your lot my friends, make it last."

"Don't worry about that," said Webster, finally recovering his breath. He raised the glass up to the light and peered at the clear liquid. "I think a second glass of this would kill me. It's not exactly The Macallan is it? Or even a Lagavulin, although it is foul enough."

Jones leaned further over the table and lowered his voice. "It is indeed. But I think a Red Army Sergeant should probably avoid discussing the finer points of single malt. A little out of character, don't you think?"

Webster blanched. "Sorry Major."

"Don't worry about it, but please think a little harder before you speak. That goes for all of you – listen more than you talk." The others nodded, faces serious.

"Spread out. Start some conversation. Buy your new comrades a couple of drinks. But don't go overboard, you're supposed to be poorly-paid soldiers. See if you can find out anything about the train or the mine, anything that might be useful."

Jones looked at them each in turn. "Be back at the freight yard in two hours. Anyone who doesn't make the rendezvous, I'm sorry, you're on your own."

Fitzgerald shuffled in his seat. "And what if you're the one who doesn't make it back Major?"

"I'm touched by your concern Fitz, but I figure there's more to it than that. Still worried about your ride home are you?"

"Obviously. Who wouldn't be? I don't want to be stuck here simply because you were too bloody pig-headed to tell us before you got yourself killed."

Jones considered for a moment and then relented. "A fair point. From tomorrow, for the next three nights, our friend Wilberforce will have his airship waiting for us beyond the ridge to the north of the mine. He'll arrive at midnight each night and stay for two hours. If he doesn't see the signal, he leaves."

"What's the signal?" asked Webster.

"A flare or a fire, a mile to the south of where we want picked up."

Webster looked confused. "Why not pick us up at the flare?"

"Because although the area should be deserted, I don't think Wilberforce fancies inadvertently dropping in on any wandering Bolshies having a campfire sing-song."

"Ah, yes. One sees his point."

"And what happens after the third night Major?" asked Fitzgerald.

"After three nights, that's it. After that, if you still want out of Russia, you walk."

Kowalski lifted his glass. "Here's to us all catching our ride. I've had enough walking in the snow to last a lifetime." All four clinked their glasses together and took a sip, even Webster.

Jones pushed his chair back and stood. "See you all in a couple of hours Comrades." He turned and made his way into the throng. With a nod to each other, the rest moved off.

*

Kowalski made his way round the crowded bar, observing its patrons. As he stood in the corner near the stove, he spotted a likely prospect. The Russian sergeant was looking flushed and a little tipsy, but wasn't roaring drunk. Even better, he was moving back and forth between two different groups of soldiers – perfect. If Kowalski managed to engage him in conversation, then neither group would pay much attention. He had decided he would deliberately bump into the man the next time he passed. An offer to buy a drink by way of apology would serve as a good introduction.

However, before he could act on his plan, he felt a hand on his arm. It was Jones. "Comrade Captain, I need you outside. Now."

Kowalski followed Jones through the packed crowd and out of the door. They climbed the creaking steps to street level, gratefully pulling in deep breaths of the fresh air, pleased to be out of the fug of the bar. Whilst they had been inside it had started to snow and now fat, heavy flakes swirled through the patches of lamplight.

They marched off down the street together, Jones setting a brisk pace. Kowalski took a good look around, checking they were alone. "What's the story Major?" he asked, dropping back into English for the first time since they had left the freight yard earlier.

"We need to get back to the hut, sharpish."

"Why?"

"I'll explain later. I need to think."

Kowalski was doing some thinking himself: thinking perhaps Fitzgerald was right, sometimes Jones did keep his cards too close to his chest. Still, he hadn't got them killed just yet, and that counted for a lot in Kowalski's books. All the same, he loosened the flap on his pistol holster and scanned the streets carefully for any signs of observation or pursuit. Jones was clearly worried about something, and the Major didn't strike him as the type to worry easily. Kowalski decided he would worry too, even if he had no idea what he was supposed to be worried about.

*

The freight yard looked as deserted as before, but Jones still waited a good five minutes, watching from the dark pools of shadow between the flickering streetlamps. Only when he was sure no welcoming committee awaited did they proceed towards the hut. Once inside, the Englishman moved quickly to the desk and swept the jumble of wires away from the telegraph unit. He turned a dial and the silver wheels immediately shifted alignment.

"Telegram from the Queen?" asked Kowalski.

"I'm not quite old enough to be getting one of those yet. Keep an eye out would you?"

Jones read quickly through the messages the telegraph had stored whilst they were out in town. At this time of night, communication traffic was light and it didn't take him long to find what he was looking for. Thankfully the message out of Cheka headquarters had only been sent in the last few minutes. They might have a bit of time after all.

He tapped out a reply on the spring-loaded switch and flicked the machine to transmit. Abandoning the desk, he started rummaging through the stowed gear by the light of the small electric lamp, transferring items from one pack to another.

Satisfied, he straightened up. “Right. That will have to do.”

Hefting a bulging pack onto each shoulder, he made for the door. “I’m off out again. Shan’t be long. Should be back before anyone else arrives.”

“And I suppose I stay here?”

“Yes please.”

“Whatever you say Major,” replied Kowalski as Jones ventured out into the night.

*

The fire had gone out, but the stove was still warm to the touch. Kowalski found he could perch on it and see out into the yard through the gap in the blind. As he waited for Jones to return, the heat in the metal beneath him slowly worked its way through his various layers. Twice now this little stove had made him warm and happy. Kowalski thought he might have finally found true love.

At the faint crunch of a footfall in the snow outside, he abandoned his cosy seat and padded across the room to stand behind the door, raising his silenced pistol.

“Kowalski,” whispered Jones’ voice, “It’s me. Don’t bloody shoot me.” The door opened and Jones slipped in, brushing snow from his shoulders. The two packs were nowhere to be seen.

“Right then. All set outside. Time to arrange a little surprise in here.”

Jones placed the carbine on the table and began fiddling with the weapon. Kowalski returned to his perch on the stove. "Major, I hate to sound like Fitz, but is there any chance you could give me a single clue as to what the hell is going on?"

"You will not be in the dark much longer Captain, I promise. Here, take this," said Jones, tossing Kowalski a roll of wire and gesturing toward the other room. "Run this through there and climb out that window. Wait for me outside."

Once they were both out in the cold, Jones carefully slid the window back down, leaving a small gap for the wire. Playing out the cable behind them, they moved out into the darkness of the yard, heading for a group of freight cars about thirty feet from the building. Dropping to their knees, the two men crawled beneath one of the rail trucks.

When Kowalski squeezed in beside Jones he found they had a good view round the side of the hut and back toward the faint lights of the street at the edge of the yard. Jones lay alongside the packs he had obviously stowed here earlier, clutching the wire they had run from the hut.

As Kowalski hunkered down, Jones handed him another length of cable. "On my signal, give this a tug. There's a good chap."

Kowalski got as comfortable as he could on the frozen stones between the rail tracks. Settled, he turned his head and whispered, "I'm assuming from all this that you're expecting company?"

"Well deduced Captain. Unless I'm very much mistaken, this yard will shortly be crawling with our Russian friends."

"You think the others got caught?"

"Caught. Or something else."

Lying on the freezing ground in the middle of hostile territory, apparently waiting for half the Red Army to show up, Kowalski was in no mood for mysterious hints. "Come on Major, spill the beans. What did you read on that machine?"

Before Jones could answer, the night's quiet was shattered by shouting and the pounding of feet from the opposite side of the yard. Above the general clamour rose a dreadful and familiar mechanical racket. The shapes of men with guns materialised between the freight cars, but beyond them, lurching forward with clanking, squealing steps, they made out the formidable bulk of a walker. It towered over the yard, snow swirling around its metal frame. The walker stomped between the rail trucks before crunching to a halt, turning its armoured body so the cannon barrel pointed straight at the hut which Jones and Kowalski had so recently vacated.

A searchlight atop the walker blazed out, casting long shadows from the twenty Soviet soldiers who now surrounded the building, weapons raised. Where the light struck snow, it reflected up, hard and bright. The yard became a monochrome world of dazzling whites and inky, dangerous blacks.

An amplified voice, crackling in heavily-accented English, echoed out. "Come out of there. Immediately." The order echoed round the yard.

"They ain't messing about Major. What do we do now?"

Jones gave him a hard grin. "What else? We pick a fight. Head down Captain." The Englishman gave the wire in his fist a sharp yank.

The harsh chatter of the carbine burst from the hut, the tug on the wire having activated the trigger mechanism. Jones must have wedged the weapon in place, pointing towards the window and the yard outside. As the glass was shattered by the sudden fusillade from within, the surrounding soldiers threw themselves to the ground or sought cover behind the trucks.

After a moment of disarray, the Russians began returning fire. The crack of rifles was joined by the sharp repeating bark of the walker's mechanised gun. The hut visibly shook under the impact of hundreds of bullets, snow sliding from the trembling roof tiles.

"Jesus," said Kowalski, "I'm glad we ain't in there."

"But hopefully our Bolshevik friends are convinced that we are," Jones replied. "Time for us to become a couple of ghosts. Give that wire a tug."

Kowalski did as instructed, pulling hard. The night erupted in noise and flame.

The explosives blew the dilapidated building into matchwood. The blast knocked Russian soldiers from their feet and showered them with debris. A hot wave of air rolled outward, its warmth reaching the two men beneath the freight car as clumps of soil and chunks of wood began clattering back to earth. A fat, greasy fireball rolled upwards into the sky as it became clear the hut was gone, replaced with a burning pile of rubble. That poor little stove, thought Kowalski.

"Haul in the cable," whispered Jones.

They pulled in the wires as the Russians began picking themselves up from the ground. Confused soldiers staggered around in the smoke attempting to shake off the concussion of the blast. One man, greatcoat on fire and arms flailing, was pushed back down and rolled in the snow by his fellows. From the hatch on top of the walker, a Russian officer began yelling panicked orders which were duly ignored by the stunned troops below. The prone figures nearest the wreckage remained still, either unconscious or dead.

Jones tugged at Kowalski's arm and he dragged his eyes away from the chaotic scene. "Come on. Let's get out of here while the Bolshies are distracted."

Dragging the bags behind them, they squeezed out from under the rail car. They picked their way round the fringes of the yard, keeping in the shadows of the trucks cast by the fire, heading for the engine shed. Crossing the tracks in front of the locomotive's curved snowplough, they put the dark bulk of the engine between themselves and the soldiers.

They ignored the engine footplate and the passenger cars and headed down the train towards the coal trucks at the rear. Jones clambered up onto the last car and peered over the side.

"Hop up Captain. Here's our ride."

"Nothing a little warmer Major?" asked Kowalski as he climbed aboard. The hopper was a metal box designed to swing over and dump its cargo of coal. Currently empty, it was about five feet deep, and filthy.

"Sadly no. It's not exactly the Orient Express, is it?"

"You can say that again." He eyed the inside of the truck with distaste as he dropped into the interior. "Webster would be appalled."

"A little dust never hurt anyone. And it definitely beats walking."

"There is that," said Kowalski, sitting wearily down on his pack. "Now Major, you really need to tell me what the hell is going on."

"Yes. I probably do. I've kept you in the dark for a little too long I think."

"Heh. Now there's an understatement."

"Very well," began Jones, shifting to get comfortable on his own pack. "We were betrayed to the Russians this evening. Betrayed by one of the men we brought with us from London."

Kowalski stared at him, speechless.

"Buckingham is convinced information has been leaking out to Russia for some time now. His investigations have narrowed the problem down to two intelligence sections."

"Webster's and Fitzgerald's?"

"Exactly. When this business with Eisenstein arose, the Duke couldn't risk any news reaching the Russians before we arrived. He figured that if we took them along it would keep our mission secret, and eventually the turncoat would reveal himself. Two birds, one stone – that sort of thing."

"So you still don't know which one of them it is?"

"No. The telegraph message I intercepted only used a codename."

"And where do I fit into this picture Major?"

"You're here as the only man I can trust." Jones puffed out his cheeks. "I'm sorry I haven't brought you up to speed sooner Captain. But I couldn't risk you behaving differently towards our friends. It was important our traitor believed he remained unsuspected."

"So that stuff about getting a drink and gathering information earlier? That was all baloney?"

"I was giving our friend the opportunity to seek out his secret police chums. Now with us apparently dead, the Cheka should follow the orders I sent them. We tag along as stowaways, hopefully identifying our man, and getting us into the mine facility." He shrugged. "Two birds, one stone."

"Just like that?"

"It's an unorthodox plan I know, but it's the best I could come up with."

Kowalski tipped his head back and rested it on the cold steel of the truck. "Major, it ain't unorthodox, it's unbelievable."

*

Commander Baburin, the head of the Murmansk branch of the Cheka, slipped a fingertip under the felt of his eye patch and rubbed at the scar tissue beneath. He closed his good eye and leaned back in his chair, taking a draw of his cigarette and taking stock of his conflicting emotions.

It appeared he had captured a ring of Imperial saboteurs bent on the destruction of one of the country's most important scientific endeavours. However, the fact remained the infiltrators had penetrated to the heart of his jurisdiction without him being any the wiser. And he himself had seemingly spoken with the ringleader in the square earlier in the day. Intolerable.

He had been worried that rather than providing his ticket out of this frozen purgatory, this incident would see him moving onward to a gulag cell somewhere even colder. Thankfully, it seemed his Moscow superiors were taking a positive view of Baburin's most recent communiqué. Perhaps his achievement would be brought to the attention of Comrade Felix himself, the wily old head of the Cheka. He stubbed out his smoke and picked up the telegraph message again, barely managing to suppress the smile twitching at the corner of his mouth as he read.

Your captive is who he claims to be. Allow him to make his way home. Take the others to the General for interrogation and then send them on to Moscow.

Well done Comrade Commander.

Baburin's reading was interrupted as the Englishman was ushered into the room. He indicated a chair and told the guard to remove the captive's shackles.

"My apologies for doubting you Comrade, but I'm sure you can understand my need to verify your credentials."

The man visibly relaxed as he sank into his seat. "Of course. Perhaps now you can get me a drink? Some brandy, or a whisky. Anything but vodka."

Baburin disliked the tone of command, but figured he would humour the Englishman. He had, after all, done Baburin's career a power of good this night. The occasion called for something special. The Russian opened his desk drawer and pulled a bottle of whisky from within. Earlier in the month it had been confiscated from a steamer captain caught smuggling decadent luxuries into the country. He signalled to the guard to fetch two glasses from a cupboard and when they were delivered he motioned for the soldier to leave.

He poured out two measures of the amber liquid. "How are you to return to England? Our superiors are keen for you to take up your former duties once again."

The Englishman took a sip, sighing in contentment. "There's an airship coming at midnight for the next three nights. The pickup area is to the north of the mine."

Baburin glanced at the clock. Dawn was still hours away.

"We will take you out to the mine later this morning. The General will want to debrief you in person, and I'm sure he will want to speak to your compatriots."

Baburin was relishing the moment when he revealed the captured spies to the army man. General Gorev usually treated the secret police and its Commander with disdain, resenting the control the Cheka's Political Commisars exercised over his officers. He could have cabled the mine with his news, but had decided to deliver the information in person. It promised to be a most satisfying morning.

The Russian raised his glass. "Tonight you will be on your way back to London, the sole survivor of a failed mission."

"Not before you've captured Jones and the American. If I return to London claiming they're dead, I cannot very well afford for them to turn up alive and well. I need to see them in chains before I board that airship."

"I am awaiting news, although I cannot imagine there will be any problems. I sent twenty of my best men and a walker."

"Don't underestimate them, Commander. From what I've seen they're both extremely capable."

They were interrupted by a knock at the door and a mousy secretary snuck in, note in hand. Baburin took it and dismissed her with a backhanded wave as he looked it over. He raised an eyebrow as he read.

"Well Comrade, it appears they were not that capable after all. Your friends are dead."

"You're sure of this?"

"My men moved in and there was an exchange of fire. The building exploded. There was a fire. Nobody came out." Baburin passed the note across the desk. "A shame we now only have one Imperial spy to interrogate, but at least your story will contain a greater element of truth."

The Englishman slumped back in his chair and shook his head slowly. "Jones took on a platoon of men and a walker? Typical – bravery and stupidity in equal measure."

Baburin laughed and raised his drink in a toast. "Long may such Imperial stupidity continue, eh Comrade Webster?"

The traitor smiled, lifting his own glass. "I'll drink to that."

Part Two

As dawn broke, the train became the focus of increasing activity, the tramp of feet and shouted orders echoing under the engine shed's roof. Jones and Kowalski heard the sounds of the locomotive being prepared for service – the shovelling of coal and the rising hiss of steam pressure. Whenever voices or footsteps sounded near their end of the train, the two men crouched as low as they could in the steel hopper, unconsciously holding their breath.

Despite their unspoken fears, the closest they came to discovery was when a passing soldier threw his cigarette butt into their truck. As the glowing ember sailed unannounced over the side and landed between them, both men had jumped with shock. They had shared nervous smiles after the smoker had stomped off.

They listened now to the arrival of a troop of soldiers. As the marching feet came to a halt, the doors on the passenger cars clattered. The soldiers boarding for the change of security detail at the mine, thought Jones. He resisted the urge to peer over the top of the coal truck to see if he could catch a glimpse of any other passengers. He was desperate to see if he could recognise either Fitzgerald or Webster, but the risk of someone in the shed spotting him was too great. Identifying the traitor would have to wait.

Of course, they might not even be on the train. It was a fair assumption the two men would be taken out to the mine for the General's attention, but it was by no means a certainty. Jones clamped down hard on this line of thinking. No use in second-guessing himself now. There was nothing he could do about it. They would be aboard or they would not – only time would tell.

A long shrill whistle sounded from the locomotive. As the note faded, the train jerked into motion and they pulled slowly out of the shed.

Kowalski leaned forward. “Thank God we’re on the move. I was starting to go a little crazy.”

“Don’t get too excited. It’s still an hour’s journey to the mine and it’s going to be bloody cold.”

“Nothing new there Major.”

But Kowalski was wrong. The train journey introduced them to a whole new level of cold, unlike anything they had experienced so far.

As the train picked up speed, the wind whistled into the open truck, chilling the two stowaways to the bone. They pulled the flaps of their fur hats close about their faces and crouched against the forward wall of the hopper seeking what little shelter it afforded. Any small desire either man harboured to see the passing countryside was overwhelmed by the awful thought of lifting his head above the rim and exposing his face to the bitter wind.

They huddled together for meagre comfort as time stretched out in a haze of cold and cramp and chattering teeth. Jones felt like he had been stuck in this freezing metal coffin for an eternity. To make things worse, snow began to fall from the leaden skies once again, adding damp to the misery.

At last though, as he was beginning to drift off into a numb state of shock, he felt the vibration through his feet lessen, and the bite of the wind began to ease slightly. The train was finally slowing down.

He flexed his frozen joints. “Here we are Captain. Time to risk a little look.”

Avoiding any sudden movement they raised their heads, a fraction of an inch at a time, until they could just see over the side of their truck.

The train was rolling on at barely more than walking pace. Ahead of them, and opening now to allow their passage, was a gate of thick planks bound with iron. It provided the only access through a high stone wall crowned with spikes, running off in either direction. Jones was relieved at the lack of watchtowers. That had been his primary worry, that a guard with a raised vantage point would glance down and spot the two infiltrators crouched in the coal truck. The guards on the gate were safely on the ground, unable to see into the hopper.

Outside the wall, to the right of the rail tracks, a work party of shaven-headed prisoners leaned on shovels and picks, stealing a respite from their digging as their overseers turned to watch the train roll in. The pit they were covering over with soil was deep, but Jones and Kowalski could still see the thin frozen limbs of the corpses reaching up to the sky from beneath the dirt. The two men in the coal truck looked at each other, eyes cold and hard. Without words they agreed, someone would pay for this.

Beyond the gate the rails curved round in a wide spiral descending into a natural bowl-shaped depression. They went on to form a circular loop of track half a mile in diameter, running through clusters of cranes, loading towers and low wooden buildings. Within the space enclosed by the rails, conveyor belt systems climbed from heaps of earth and coal, and huge shovel-tractors spewed steam and smoke as they moved back and forth. Across from their vantage point, beyond a station platform, Jones saw a pair of huge steel doors hanging open to reveal a tunnel heading back into the hill. The laboratories were in there, he thought, remembering the smuggled drawings Hanson had shown them days earlier. That was where Eisenstein would be.

At the centre of the depression, towering above everything else, four pylons rose. Mounted between them on enormous gears was a steel cylinder, perhaps forty feet in diameter, its surface covered with a tangled network of pipes and vents. The base of the cylinder tapered to a point in tiers of jagged metallic teeth. Directly below the fearsome drill gaped the mouth of the mine itself, a perfectly round hole matching the proportions of the cylinder above and disappearing straight down, its black void contrasting starkly with the snow-covered ground.

The two men dropped back into concealment as their truck approached the gate. Jones was sure no noise would carry over the clacking rhythm of the wheels but he still waited until they were safely through and past the guards before he spoke.

"When the train stops we should be perfectly placed to hop out and get into cover."

Kowalski crossed his arms over his chest, pushing his gloved hands into his armpits. "As long as we ain't in this icebox for a moment longer than we need to be, that's fine by me Major."

The train proceeded slowly round the spiral, descending into the bowl through the falling snow. With a long hiss of steam and the squeal of brakes, the locomotive slowed. The train came to a halt with the two passenger cars lined up alongside the station platform in front of the tunnel. The coal trucks stretched out behind amidst the boilers, pipes and cranes.

With the banging of doors and the shouting of the officers, the passenger cars began to empty. Jones moved to the other side of their truck, away from the activity. With a quick check they were unobserved, he clambered up and over quickly, dropping to the icy ground, stiff knees complaining as they absorbed the impact. Kowalski joined him, crouching beside the track.

Staying low, the two men shuffled quickly away from the train, into the cover of a twisted forest of piping and valves. They took shelter beside a large steel boiler, its girth concealing them from the tunnel entrance, and the jumble of pipes and machinery around it preventing any casual discovery from other directions.

The boiler's riveted plating was piping hot and both men sat with their backs pressed gratefully against it. Slowly the numbing cold of the journey was driven out of their torsos by the boiler's heat, and after a few minutes even their fingers and toes began tingling back into life.

"Now we're thawed out slightly, I think it's time to prepare some surprises for our friend Ivan." Jones patted the pack by his side. "Time to distribute some of the little presents we brought with us from England. How are you with gift deliveries Captain?"

Kowalski raised his hand and adopted a solemn tone. "Neither snow, nor rain, nor gloom of night shall stay this courier from the swift completion of his appointed rounds."

Jones stared at him, baffled.

"Heh. I got an Uncle in the Postal Service."

Jones was still confused.

"Forget it Major. I'll explain it over a beer sometime. What's the plan?"

"We split up. I'll head around the outside, putting a charge on anything that looks expensive. We meet up back here."

"What do you want me to do?"

"See that bloody great drill thing? I thought we might break it. Think you could manage that Captain?"

"Just watch me Major," said Kowalski with a smile. "Breaking things is what you folks are paying me for. What kind of timing are we putting on the fuses?"

Jones checked his pocket watch. "Let's start the party at noon. That gives us three hours to find Eisenstein and his daughter. Should be plenty of time."

"These shitty Soviet timers you insisted on will run at different speeds. Over three hours we could end up with a bit of a spread."

"A spread will be fine. Keeps things lively. As the Bolshies respond to one blast, another will knock them sideways." He stood, hoisting his pack onto his shoulder. "Right, I'm off. I'll see you on the other side."

*

"Good morning Comrade General," said Baburin.

General Gorev lifted his head from a desk strewn with technical drawings and papers of scribbled equations. The man was something of a contradiction. With his bulky frame and bulging muscles, he certainly didn't look like a scientist, and the Cheka man knew Gorev spent as much time in the gymnasium as he did in his laboratories.

The General's lip curled in distaste when he recognised his visitor. "What is it this time Baburin?"

"A matter of state security."

The army man sneered, "Isn't it always? Another ship's captain and his unlicensed alcohol?"

"Forgive me, perhaps I should have gone straight to the Comrade Director in Moscow, rather than interrupting your, ah, mathematics." Gorev's eyes narrowed, but Baburin continued before he could interrupt. "But as military governor of the region, you should know I have captured a band of Imperialist agents, bent on interrupting your precious enterprise."

Baburin felt a fierce satisfaction at the look on the General's face. This moment was worth all the sneering he'd put up with from the senior officer in the past. The Army and the Cheka rarely saw eye to eye, but the General was an extreme case. He showed little interest in political security, even allowing Jews and other undesirables to work on his secret project, despite Baburin's objections. Objections that now looked all too valid.

"You have these men in custody?" The arrogance was gone from the General's tone, faded along with blood from his face. The shock of a threat to his endeavours had cut through his confidence.

"One of them was captured, another two are dead. All thanks to the work of a Chekist agent, a hero of the people."

"Their objective?"

"To sabotage your efforts here at the mine, and to spirit away their man on the inside."

"What man? What are you talking about?" The General looked close to panic now. Imperialist agents were one thing, but a security issue within his own staff was another matter entirely. A matter for the Cheka.

"The Jew. Eisenstein. The one I warned you about. He is an Imperialist traitor."

Gorev rubbed at his temples. "And you have proof of all this?"

Of course I have proof you idiot, Baburin wanted to scream, but much as he had the upper hand over the Army man at the moment, it wouldn't be wise to push too hard. Gorev was a powerful man, both physically and politically. If the mood took him, the General could break Baburin in either fashion.

"I brought the two Englishmen with me. I assumed you would wish to speak with them."

The General got to his feet. He adjusted his cuffs and smoothed down the front of his uniform tunic. "You assume correctly. I will summon Eisenstein too. If what you say is correct then he must face the consequences of his betrayal." He drummed his fingers on the desk. "I cannot afford to execute him, regardless of his crimes. It would not do to waste such a mind." He smiled. "Perhaps I will make him watch as his daughter loses an eye."

Baburin winced, resisting the urge to rub at his scar. "Or she could provide some entertainment for your soldiers?"

The General nodded. "Crude and unsophisticated, but perhaps effective. We shall see how he reacts when we confront him with the failure of the Imperial saboteurs. If he begs for mercy, an eye. If he is defiant, the troops." He paused for a moment before looking at Baburin. "Good work Comrade Commander."

That must have hurt, thought Baburin. He was unable to

recall the last time Gorev had accorded him or his rank any respect. He could almost feel the warmth of a new posting in Moscow.

*

With his charges set and his pack considerably lighter, Jones cut across the mine workings and made for the train. He headed for the locomotive at its front and pulled himself up onto the footplate.

The cab's forward wall was a mass of gauges, valves and levers, broken up by the open hatch of the firebox, glowing coals visible within. Before this welcome heat an engineer sat on an upturned bucket, warming his hands. The man looked up at his visitor, face streaked black beneath his filthy cap.

"Good morning Comrade," said Jones. "Do you mind if I borrow some of your warmth?"

The engineer waved him in towards the heat. "Help yourself. Nobody else is using it."

Jones moved in beside the man and pulled his gloves off, rubbing his hands together. "Ah," he breathed, "that is good. You are a lucky man Comrade. You must have the only warm job in the whole of Siberia."

The man shrugged. "Maybe. Gets a sight too warm when we have to get moving. Nothing beats the chill like shovelling coal."

Jones nodded in agreement. "I don't envy you that task." He lifted his gaze to take in the controls. "However, I do envy you that you get to drive this magnificent machine. Although how you work out which lever does what, that would be beyond me."

"Ah, it's not so difficult." The engineer tapped the side

of his nose and leaned forward conspiratorially. "We railwaymen like to make it look complicated, you know." He barked out a laugh. "Keeps us in a job."

Jones gave him a smile. "Just like soldiering. We like to make it look harder than it really is." He pulled out his cigarette case and offered it to the other man. The engineer took one and then reached for a pair of tongs, lifting a small coal out of the firebox and holding it so he and Jones could light their smokes. He took his first draw, and puffed in obvious pleasure.

"These are good. Better than the usual shit we get round here."

"I'm lucky. I have a friend in Moscow who keeps me in decent tobacco. When he can get hold of it, that is."

"Very lucky, to have friends such as those," said the engineer, taking another deep draw.

Jones indicated the controls around them. "So, if I promise not to tell anyone the secrets of your craft, would you tell me how you drive this thing?"

The engineer smiled. "Like I said, it's simple really..."

Five minutes and another cigarette later, Jones climbed down from the footplate and headed for his rendezvous with Kowalski.

*

They walked through the falling snow along the station platform, past a huddle of soldiers clustered around a glowing brazier. Kowalski resisted the nervous urge to whistle. He had always believed it was vastly over-rated as a marker of innocence, convinced guards the world over were sent to special training schools where they were taught to be doubly-suspicious of anyone whistling. Besides, the only Russian tune he could think of at the moment was Tchaikovsky's 1812. Not exactly whistling material.

Stomping up the steps from the platform, they came to the wide paved area in front of the tunnel. A pair of steel doors, a full ten feet high, stood open at the entrance to the underground complex. Jones gave the guard at the doors a nod and the man returned a lacklustre salute, more interested in shuffling around trying to stay warm than in the comings and goings of senior officers.

The two men passed through the entrance, into the side of the hill. The tunnel was round, clearly bored by some smaller sibling of the giant drill outside. Kowalski was surprised to find the rock walls dry, he realised he had been expecting some kind of dank hole. They marched down the slight slope for about fifty feet before bulkhead doors began punctuating the rough walls to either side. Electric lamps were strung from the roof above, gradually taking over illumination duties from the weak light filtering in from outside. A mix of soldiers and civilians bustled about but paid no attention to the two newcomers.

Kowalski leaned towards Jones. "This place is pretty big Major. A regular rabbit warren. You know where the Professor and his daughter will be?"

"They both have offices on the fifth level down. Here's hoping they're hard at work this morning..."

Two hundred feet in, the tunnel opened up into a wider space, criss-crossed with the metal struts and cabling of the elevator system. Thick metal poles, slick with grease, formed two shafts for the passenger cages and their counterweights. These central cores were surrounded by a framework of girders anchored to the rock walls, supporting a wooden staircase that disappeared down into the darkness. As Jones and Kowalski waited, the cables sang and a large counterweight block sailed downwards. One of the elevators was on its way up.

The cage arrived with a metallic clash and the concertina gate was slid open by the overalled man within. He nodded to the two waiting men and stepped out of the elevator, pulling a trolley cart laden with rock samples. He didn't give them a second glance as he wheeled his load up the tunnel.

The infiltrators stepped into the elevator cage and pulled the gate shut. As Jones moved the lever on the control console to select the fifth level, Kowalski looked down, immediately wishing he hadn't. Beneath the soles of his boots and the thin metal strips of the mesh floor, he could see struts and girders caught in occasional patches of light, framing a deep, square darkness that seemed to descend into infinity.

He felt a moment of sickening vertigo and thrust a hand out to grab the railing running round the inside of the cage. Ridiculous. He couldn't be scared of heights: he jumped out of airships for a living. Somehow this was different though – the shaft was a cramped and claustrophobic abyss, unlike the wide, rushing freedom of a drop. As the elevator jerked into action and began shuddering its way down, Kowalski clenched the rail until his knuckles were white.

"How far down does this thing go?" he asked, unsure if he wanted to know the answer.

Jones glanced at the console. "Seven levels."

The first floor slid past in splash of light. Twenty or thirty feet between floors, reckoned Kowalski, doing calculations in his head. A couple of hundred feet? A fraction of the altitudes he'd cheerfully dropped from. Annoyed and amused with himself in equal measure, he made a conscious effort to relax his grip on the rail and breathe deeply, inwardly counting the floors as they passed. He grew calmer, but resisted any urge to look down again.

*

The elevator juddered to a halt and Jones slid the gate open. They stepped out of the cage and found themselves standing in a semicircular chamber carved out of the bare rock, the straight side taken up by the steel framework of the elevators shaft at their backs. In the centre of the curved rock facing them was a metal door, a match for the ones they had seen on the upper level. They moved towards it and Jones took a quick look through the thick glass of the porthole mounted above the wheel.

"One guard. I'll do the talking, but get that pop gun of yours ready, just in case..."

He placed his hands on the locking wheel as Kowalski attached the brass suppressor cylinder to the barrel of his pistol. When the Floridian nodded in readiness, Jones spun the wheel and swung the heavy door inwards.

They ducked through the doorway and entered the corridor beyond. The air was warmer in here and the walls were smooth, unlike the rock surfaces they had seen up until now. The walls were painted too, an institutional shade of magnolia, although it seemed a dazzling white at first as their eyes adjusted to the stronger lighting in this section of the complex. The corridor ran on, wooden doors on either side, frosted glass panels painted with numbers and names. Only the lack of windows and the soldier sitting behind the desk in the hallway suggested this was anything other than a normal office building.

The guard looked up as they entered, frowning slightly as he took in their dishevelled uniforms. Clearly this area of the facility was not often frequented by soldiers who had spent the night in a coal truck. Nonetheless, the new arrivals outranked him, so he stood and gave a salute, despite their appearance.

"Comrade Major, Comrade Captain, what can I do for you?"

Jones stepped up to the desk and returned the salute. "The General wishes to speak with Professor Eisenstein. We have been sent to escort him upstairs."

The guard looked confused. "The Jew? Two men already came and took him away."

Damn it, thought Jones. He gave the guard a rueful smile. "Typical. They collected the wrong Eisenstein. They were supposed to bring the daughter. If they've already taken the Professor then we shall make do with the girl. Where is she?"

"The girl? Not sure I'd call her that. Not to her face anyway." He gestured over his shoulder with his thumb. "She's in her office. But I'll need to see your passes before I can let you back there."

Jones gave an apologetic shrug. "We don't have any yet. We've only just arrived and the General sent us straight down here." He indicated his dirty uniform. "Didn't even give us time to change."

The guard frowned. "Forgive me Comrade Major, but I will have to check. It will only take a moment." He reached for the telephone apparatus standing on the desk.

Jones winced, silently cursing the man's dedication to his duty. "Captain..." he said, taking a step to the side.

There was a muffled crack and a small round hole appeared in the guard's pale forehead. The soldier crumpled to the floor, lifeless. Kowalski stuffed his pistol back into the pocket of his greatcoat and went to lift the body.

"Some folks are just too damned keen on following orders."

"Quite. What shall we do with him?"

Kowalski indicated a nearby door, 'Fire' labelled across it in bright red Cyrillic lettering.

"Perfect," said Jones, reaching for the dead man's feet.

They were almost there, the body slung between them, when one of the doors opened further up the corridor. A young man in a dark suit emerged, a sheaf of papers in hand, and began walking down the hall towards them. Kowalski fumbled for his pistol, but the man didn't even look up from his reading as he stopped at the next office down, knocked once and entered.

Jones shook his head. "Scientists, oblivious to the real world."

"I ain't complaining," muttered Kowalski.

They stuffed the corpse in amongst the fire-fighting equipment, Jones pulling the dead man's weapon from its holster and pocketing it. As he straightened up from the body, the Russian's head rolled back, and Jones found himself looking into the guard's frozen expression of surprise.

"Sorry about that old chap," he said as he pulled the door closed.

*

Two-thirds of the way down the long corridor, they found the office they were looking for. The frosted glass panel in the door read 'Dr M Eisenstein'.

"Doctor, huh? And a Professor for a Pa. Well ain't they the clever family?"

"Obviously. Let's introduce ourselves to the good doctor, shall we?" Jones gave the glass a rap with his knuckles and turned the handle without waiting for a response.

The office was small and cramped, an impression magnified by the heaps of books and papers piled on every surface. The walls were taken up with overflowing bookshelves and blackboards covered in a chalked scrawl of equations and diagrams. Behind a cluttered desk sat a woman, her long dark hair pulled messily back in a loose ponytail. She turned to look at the visitors, leaping to her feet when she spotted the uniforms.

She had a face Kowalski would not exactly have described as beautiful, but she was certainly striking. He would have placed a sizeable bet there and then on her having a wonderful smile, but it became immediately apparent there no hope of seeing it at the moment.

"What are you doing in here? Where is my father? What have you done with him?"

Jones raised both his hands in a placatory gesture. "Comrade Doctor, please. There is no need to shout."

If anything, the volume level increased. "No need to shout? You had no need to drag my father off like some criminal. Where is he?" The woman looked like she was winding up to go on like this for some time.

"For God's sake," Jones hissed in English. "Keep your

voice down."

Shocked into silence, she looked at them both, conflicting expressions of suspicion and hope chasing one another across her face.

"Who are you?" she asked in heavily accented English, her tone quieter but no softer.

Before Jones could answer, there came a sharp knocking behind them. Kowalski immediately drew his pistol, but held it low, shielding it from view. The doctor's eyes widened when she saw the weapon. He gave her what he hoped was a reassuring wink.

Jones yanked the door open. "Yes?" he demanded of the civilian who stood there, arm raised mid-knock.

Taken aback, the man took a moment to recover. He licked his lips and smoothed his hand over his oiled hair, taking in the two soldiers. He lifted himself up on tiptoes to peer over Jones' shoulder. "Comrade Doctor, is everything well? I heard shouting."

The woman paused. Kowalski saw her glance down at the pistol in his hand. "Everything is fine Comrade Nevsky. Go back to your office. I was just trying to find out where these brutes have taken my father."

The man in the doorway grimaced. "Be careful Maria. You would do well to distance yourself from the old man now. His opinions have already placed you in a questionable position." He puffed out his chest. "If you wish, I could go to the General directly. He will speak with me. Then you would not have to deal with these, ah, more junior officers."

"Thank you Comrade, but I can handle this. And I shall not be distancing myself from my father either. Not for

Party favour, nor for any other reason."

The scientist's lip curled. "Such an attitude could cost you dearly Comrade. You would do well to remember that when your father, ah, retires –"

As Nevsky spoke, Kowalski saw the doctor draw breath and narrow her eyes, clearly preparing herself to tear strips from the other man. Just what they didn't need, a shouting match. Jones must have seen the same, for he interrupted the scientist, grabbing his shoulder roughly and turning him about.

"Thank you for your concern Comrade. I'm sure the doctor appreciates it. Now, on your way."

Jones ushered the man out and closed the door firmly in his outraged face. Nevsky's shadow was visible through the frosted glass as he stood outside, clearly deliberating if he should object to being manhandled out. After a moment, he turned and moved off.

The doctor shook her head. "Poor Nevsky. If only his scientific ability matched his ambition. There is one man who would not be sorry if my father were to disappear."

"That's what we're here for ma'am," said Kowalski. "To help you and the Professor disappear."

"You will forgive me if I don't believe you straight away. There was to be a token of proof..." She trailed off, looking expectantly at the two men.

Jones fished into a pocket and removed a small package wrapped in oilskin. He untied the string and handed it over. The doctor took the parcel from his hand, fingers trembling as she unwrapped it.

Kowalski leaned forward and whispered to Jones. "More secrets Major? If I didn't know you better, I'd have hurt feelings."

The woman pulled out a small black book from the folds of oilskin and held it up, tears welling in her eyes. "You know what this is?"

Jones nodded. "Your mother's diary. Your father sent it to my superiors."

"I must admit I never thought I'd see it again."

"Well, I'm not sorry to disappoint you Doctor Eisenstein. And that means it's time to leave."

Maria Eisenstein's face broke into a broad smile. Bingo, thought Kowalski, he'd have won that bet. He stepped forward and offered his hand, sweeping his fur hat from his head.

"Pleased to make your acquaintance ma'am. Captain John Kowalski, of the Floridian Free Fleet. I am at your service."

Jones rolled his eyes. "And I'm Major David Jones. I work for the British government."

The doctor looked like she couldn't believe all this was really happening. "How did you get here? I mean, into Russia? Into the mine?"

"A long story that will have to wait. We're on a tight schedule. You need to take us to your father's laboratory. I want to ensure none of his research survives what's going to happen here."

"What *is* going to happen here?"

Jones looked at her, eyes hard. "Fire and blood, Doctor."

Maria chewed at her lip. "Not all the people working here are like Nevsky. Many of them have doubts over what Bolshevism has become, they –"

"We don't have time for an ideological debate Doctor.

Personally I couldn't care less how Russia chooses to govern itself. But this bomb of yours is monstrous. It must be stopped, whatever the cost."

The doctor bristled. "This bomb of mine? How dare you? You think I had a choice in working on this?"

Jones shook his head. "Of course not. But you do now."

The anger in Maria's eyes burned itself out as Jones' words sank in. "Very well," she said quietly. "Let's go."

"I hate to remind everyone," said Kowalski, "but the clock is ticking and we still need to find the Professor."

"The Professor, and our traitor."

Maria looked confused. "Traitor? What traitor?"

"Another part of that long story. It too will have to wait. Captain Kowalski is correct, we need to get moving."

Jones reached into his pocket and pulled out the pistol he had taken from the dead guard. "Tell me, Doctor. Can you shoot?" he asked, offering her the weapon.

Maria's spark seemed to return with Jones' words. She took the pistol and clicked the magazine open, checking its contents, before shutting it with an expert flick of the wrist. "Of course I can shoot. I fought in the revolution – back when Communism was an ideal worth fighting for."

Tucking the pistol into the back of her trousers, she opened the door and strode into the hall. "Come along then," she called back over her shoulder. "I thought you were in a hurry."

Kowalski turned to Jones, a broad grin on his face. "She's a firecracker, ain't she?"

*

"How are we going to find the old man?"

Jones stopped at the guard desk and lifted the telephone.

"Why don't we call someone and ask?"

"You're kidding, right?"

"Nobody will think twice if we call to find out where to report to the General. And I figure it's a safe bet that wherever we find the General, we find the Professor."

"And Fitzgerald and Webster. And a whole heap of trigger-happy Reds too, no doubt."

As if on cue, the bulkhead door at the end of the hallway swung open and four Russian soldiers filed into the room. The leader of the new arrivals, a Sergeant, marched straight up to the desk and started to speak. Jones, playing for time, held the telephone speaker to his ear as if listening and raised an imperious finger in a silent command for the man to wait.

He spoke into the mouthpiece. "Yes, yes. Very clear, Comrade General. I will arrange it now." He hung the speaker back on its cradle.

"Comrade Major," said the Sergeant impatiently, pointing at the doctor, "I am ordered to take this woman to the General for questioning."

Jones grabbed Maria's upper arm tightly as the Sergeant spoke. Apparently making sure she wouldn't flee, in reality he was stopping her reaching for the pistol at the small of her back. She glared at him, but he simply returned her stare and gave a slight shake of his head. The three of them, armed only with pistols which none of them even had drawn, would be seriously outgunned if it came down to a firefight against soldiers carrying carbines. Jones hoped they could talk rather than shoot their way out of this one.

He turned to the Russian soldier. "Sergeant, I'm glad you've arrived. Your orders have changed. You and your men are to detain the traitor Nevsky."

"Comrade Nevsky? A traitor?"

"Indeed. Shocking, I know. A man like that, a Party man through and through – revealed as an enemy of the people." Jones leaned forward conspiratorially. "It seems he has been selling information regarding our work here to the Germans."

The Sergeant's face hardened. "Where is the bastard?"

"Still in his office, unaware his treachery has been discovered. You are to hold him there until the General arrives. Tell him nothing while he waits. Let him sweat, wondering how much we know."

The Sergeant gave a leer. "Perhaps my boys and I will soften him up a little in advance." He gestured to the doctor, still held in Jones' tight grip. "And what of the woman?"

"The Captain and I will deal with her. Where is the General?"

"Level three. The observation chamber."

"Very good. Carry on."

The soldier snapped off a salute and waved the rest of his squad over. The four Russians marched off down the hallway, whilst Jones, Kowalski and Maria made for the elevator.

"Quick thinking Major," said Kowalski as they slid the gate shut.

"Best I could come up with at short notice. I almost feel sorry for that Nevsky chap though."

"To hell with him," spat Maria. "Nevsky reported my father to that pig Baburin last year. The Cheka spent three days questioning him. All because my father had spotted a mistake in Nevsky's calculations. Bastard deserves whatever he gets."

"Heh. Remind me to never get on your wrong side Doc," said Kowalski.

She gave him a fierce smile. "Best you do not Captain. Especially now the Major has given me a pistol." She pulled the lever on the control panel and the elevator gave a jolt. Amidst a chorus of metallic groans, the cage ascended.

*

Fitzgerald found himself thinking of Moscow, assuming once they were finished with him here, he would be shipped south. Before the revolution he had visited the city many times, as both diplomat and spy. He remembered the views across the river and the stunning cathedral opposite the palace of the Kremlin. This time he knew there would be no sightseeing. He would be lucky to see anything but the inside of a cell.

The bruises he had suffered so far would be nothing compared with the treatment he'd receive at the hands of the torturers in the Russian capital. Fitzgerald knew what awaited him: mind-altering drugs which made opium look like a little pick-me-up, along with the skilled application of violence. He would eventually tell them everything. It was inevitable, although his self-respect would demand he resist them as long as he could. And then, when they were sure he could tell them no more, there would be a walk in the forest, a single bullet, and an unmarked grave.

He turned his wrists, trying to reduce the chafing from his manacles, something he supposed he would have to get used to. He was chained to one of the seats placed around a large oval table. A single lamp hung above, casting a dim light over the room's centre. The only other illumination came through the observation windows which made up the full wall down one side of the chamber. Fitzgerald could see a mass of pipes, valves, conveyor belts and pumps in the area beyond. Moving slowly around this factory, tending to the machines, were men clad in clumsy protective suits. Their domed helmets and the air flasks, coupled with the green tinge lent everything by the thick glass, made them look like deep sea divers.

He worked his tongue around his mouth, wincing as he prodded at puffed lips and loose teeth. Lifting his head, he looked across the table at the other Englishman.

"You certainly had me fooled, Webster," his hoarse voice croaked. "I would never have had you pegged as a Bolshevik. Too interested in the finer things in life to be a man of the people."

Webster smiled. "And that's the problem Fitz, don't you see it? You think the ordinary people don't deserve the finer things in life. Actually it's more than that. Your lot think the ordinary people are incapable of appreciating them."

"Your lot? What do you mean 'your lot'? My family are farmers from Staffordshire. Hardly the bloody aristocracy."

"Your family own the land which others work for their benefit. A privileged class who control the means of production." Webster shook his head. "You cannot see it, can you? That's the whole problem with capitalism."

"Whereas this," Fitzgerald gestured with his head, indicating the mine, Murmansk, the whole of Russia beyond the room, "This is utopia?"

"Of course not. Not yet. But it will be Fitz, it will be."

"Good God man. You don't really believe in all that 'Radiant Future' claptrap? Do you?"

"Why not? It's no different from your faith that British Imperialism represents progress. At least my vision of the future is one of equity and justice. At least –"

Webster's political discourse was interrupted by the opening of the chamber's heavy steel door. The guard snapped to attention as Baburin entered, followed by a tall, thickset man in the uniform of a Soviet General.

Webster leapt to his feet, eager to impress. "Pleased to meet you, Comrade General."

Gorev shook the extended hand. "And I you, Comrade. I believe I owe you my thanks. From what Comrade Commander Baburin tells me, without your intervention I could have been faced with Imperialist saboteurs disrupting my work and kidnapping my scientists. You have done Russia a great service."

Webster's eyes shone. "Anything for the good of the cause, Comrade General. It is an honour to serve the people."

The military man nodded, but Fitzgerald thought he looked uncomfortable with Webster's revolutionary zeal.

"And this one? He is one of the saboteurs?"

Baburin nodded. "The only one left alive."

The General looked down at the captive. Fitzgerald stared back, determined not to give this man the satisfaction of seeing his fear.

"Look at him Comrades," said Gorev. "Despite his chains, despite his bruises, he remains defiant. That stiff upper lip the British seem to value so highly." He patted Fitzgerald on the shoulder. "I am sure your bravery will serve you well in the cells of the Lubyanka my friend."

The metal door swung open once more and an old man was bundled into the room. Fitzgerald recognised Eisenstein from the photograph he had seen in Buckingham's office. With a jolt he realised that had only been four nights previously. It felt like an eternity ago. A different life.

The scientist recovered from his jostling, brushing at his ill-fitting suit and adjusting his glasses. He peered round at the assembled men, eyes widening as he recognised Baburin. "What is the meaning of this?" he demanded in a high-pitched voice.

The General indicated they should all take a seat around the table. Eisenstein lowered himself into the chair beside Fitzgerald, nervously taking in his bruised and swollen face. Baburin took the seat beside Webster.

Gorev sat at the head of the table, his back to the observation windows. With his broad shoulders framed against the green glow from the refinery, he leaned forward, steepling his fingers under his chin. "Well Comrades, now we are all together, what shall we talk about?"

*

Sergeant Volikov looked down at the crumpled form of Nevsky, then back up to the shocked faces of his squad. He crouched to check the man on the floor, but already knew it was pointless. They had all heard the sickening crack as the scientist's head had struck the edge of the desk on his way down.

"Damn it. I didn't even hit him that hard."

His soldiers shared nervous glances. The obvious fear was a stark, sober contrast to their previous glee at being able push around one of the uppity scientists for a change.

"Look at you lot," Volikov growled as he got to his feet. "A set of quivering women. What's the matter? Never seen a corpse before?"

"But the General..." replied one of the men, "He wanted to question him..."

"He did. Won't get any answers out of him now though, will he?"

The squad remained silent, staring at the dead man.

"Look, it's simple. Comrade Professor Nevsky tried to resist when we came to detain him, didn't he? A struggle, and an unfortunate accident. That's all." He looked at each man in turn. "Isn't that right?"

The soldiers nodded warily, clearly unconvinced. General Gorev had a notorious temper, and little patience with those who made mistakes. Volikov grew exasperated.

"You're like a bunch of frightened children. How often do the damned Cheka tell us a man died resisting arrest? This happens all the time." He gave the body a hefty kick. "Who the hell cares anyway? Bastard was a traitor. Got what he deserved."

Not just a traitor, a damned nuisance too. Imagine keeling over and dying like that. No backbone, thought Volikov. Well, not any more anyway. The Sergeant knew he'd catch some trouble for this. His men too. But he didn't think it would be too bad.

"Come on lads. Worst case, we end up with a few days of latrine duty." He slapped the youngest man on the shoulder. "Can't make Boris here smell any worse, can it?"

The others smiled weakly at the poor joke as the Sergeant opened the door and stepped out into the hallway.

Scattered heads peeked out from offices down the corridor, the scientists disturbed from their work by the noise of the brief struggle. Look at them, snorted Volikov. All spectacles and brains, not a real man amongst them. He glared at them, brows lowered in an intimidating frown perfected through years of practice on parade ground and battlefield. One by one the heads ducked back into their offices, doors closing. Whatever was happening to the unfortunate Nevsky, it was clearly none of their business.

The Sergeant turned back to his squad, still clustered around the dead man. "I'm off to make a report. You lot, stay here." He shook his head at their pale faces. "Don't let him escape, eh? Think you can manage that?"

Volikov stomped off down the passage toward the guard station at the elevators. They had one of those telephones there, he remembered. He braced himself to speak with the General.

*

The laboratories on level four were guarded in similar fashion to the offices below, but the guard on the desk recognised Maria and let the trio pass unchallenged. The walls here were made of large panes of thick glass, set in riveted metal frames, allowing a view into each of the research chambers. Following the doctor down the hallway, they passed rooms containing steel tanks stencilled with Cyrillic warning signs, and bench tables cluttered with beakers, bell-jars and gas burners.

In one of the larger rooms they saw a machine generating what could only be described as captive lightning. A shimmering, writhing electric charge squirmed in the air between two thick metal posts. Even through the glass they could hear the hiss and crackle of the raw current.

Kowalski stopped to stare, transfixed by the flickering, ever-changing shape of the harsh blue electricity. It took him a moment before he noticed the man inside the chamber. The scientist turned his head towards his observer, eyes invisible behind the black glass of his protective goggles. He raised a hand in greeting, a wave which Kowalski returned. The man turned back to his experiment, intently jotting notes down in his journal.

"What does it do?" asked Kowalksi.

"It is my father's new process," answered Maria, a note of pride in her voice. "A way to electrically separate the different types of ore. It doesn't work perfectly yet, but it is certainly beautiful."

"That it is Doc."

"Deadly too. There's enough charge flowing around in there to burn you to a cinder."

"Seems to be a lot of that round here. Don't you science folks ever build things that won't kill everyone?"

Maria glared at him. "That is rich, coming from a soldier." She strode off, stopping at the next chamber down. "My father's laboratory," she said as she swung the door open.

Inside the room the walls were covered with generators and coils of electrical equipment, no doubt connected to the lightning display next door. Down the centre of the room ran a long bench table, its surface laid with an elaborate arrangement of scientific apparatus. Kowalski looked at the collection of glass jars and tubes, burners and ceramic bowls.

He pointed at one particular piece of equipment sitting at the far end of the bench. “I won’t pretend to have a clue what all this stuff does, but I’ll be damned if that don’t look like an accordion.”

Maria gave him a withering look. Jones laughed. “It’s a bellows of some sort I think.”

“Still looks like you could get a tune out of it.”

“You’re welcome to try Captain, but first we’ll get some charges set, shall we?”

The two men worked quickly as the doctor kept watch. Within a few minutes they had rigged three of their few remaining bundles of dynamite. In a couple of hours’ time, Eisenstein’s laboratory, and a good number of the surrounding research chambers, would cease to exist in an enormous fireball. Charges set, the trio marched back through the laboratory complex, nodding to the guard at the desk as they passed on their way to the elevators.

*

Level three was unlike the other floors they had visited so far. The cage of the lift did not arrive in a lobby area here, but directly into a larger room, its walls crowded with piping and studded with gauges and control valves. The ceiling was higher in here too, allowing a gantry walkway to run round the walls. There were two metal doors in the wall before them.

“Where now doctor?” asked Jones.

“The observation chamber is on the right. The other door leads to the dressing room for the refinery workers.”

“Dressing room?”

“Protective equipment. The air in the refinery is poisonous, full of Red Mercury dust. If you take a lungful of it, you're dead in a matter of hours. A most unpleasant way to go."

They crossed the open space towards the right hand door, Jones and Kowalski drew their weapons.

"Right then," said Jones, "no time for a fancy plan. We go in as if we're escorting our prisoner. Remember, they're expecting someone to bring the doctor to them. I figure we'll have a few seconds before they realise something is not quite right. Make your first shots count."

"That's it?" asked Kowalski.

"That's it Captain. As I said, no time for a fancy plan." Jones turned to Maria. "When the shooting starts, find some cover." The doctor made to protest but Jones carried on. "Cover first, then you can get that pistol out and do as much shooting as you like."

Mollified, the doctor nodded. Jones reached for the handle of the pressure door.

"Ready..."

The air was suddenly filled with the screaming wail of an emergency klaxon, the noise reflected and magnified by the harsh metallic surfaces of the room. Into this cacophony was added the clatter of booted feet as the entrances to the gantry above were opened and soldiers poured onto the walkway.

The trio raised their pistols, but it was already too late. Six soldiers now stood around the gantry, carbines trained down on the exposed figures below. Starting a shooting match now would be suicide.

The klaxon cut out abruptly, leaving their ears ringing in the sudden silence. Jones gave the others a grim look and threw his pistol to the floor. He raised his hands in surrender, and after a moment Kowalski and Maria did the same. The noise of the door prompted them to turn. A bulky uniformed figure ducked through the portal as it swung open.

Straightening, the man looked down at Maria and gave a broad smile, although the expression did not make it as far as his eyes.

"Doctor Eisenstein, so glad you could join us." He looked at her companions. "And you brought guests too..."

He stepped to the side and gestured toward the door with a sweep of his arm.

"Come and join us. I am looking forward to making your acquaintance."

*

"And to think you told me these two were dead, Comrade Commander. They look remarkably healthy to me, no?"

Baburin shifted uncomfortably in his chair. He lifted a hand and rubbed at the scar down his cheek.

"Apparently so. I can only apologise, Comrade General."

Gorev smiled thinly. "No harm done. We have them now. Thanks to my security detail."

The Cheka officer winced, but remained silent.

Jones and Kowalski sat at the table, wrists bound with rope, an armed guard standing behind them. Maria had been brought in with them and now sat with her father, eyes downcast. Fitzgerald, still shackled to his chair, looked haunted, sunken into himself, broken. Clearly his final hope of rescue had been crushed. He slumped in silent despair.

Webster had been astonished at first, looking as if he'd

seen a pair of ghosts. However, he had soon recovered his poise as the fact of their capture had sunk in. He now smiled broadly at Jones and Kowalski across the table. The sight of him filled Jones with disgust. He followed the traitor with cold eyes as Webster got to his feet and walked over to the prisoners' equipment, piled up on the bench at the side of the room.

"Ah, here it is," he said, picking up Kowalski's brass pistol suppressor. "General, if you don't mind, I'll be taking this clever little contraption. A memento of my fallen compatriots."

"If you need a demonstration of how it works," said Kowalski in a venomous tone, "I'd be happy to oblige."

"I'm sure you would Captain, but no thank you." He turned to Jones. "You're very quiet Major. Nothing to say?"

"I'm imagining ways to make you pay for selling us to the enemy."

"I don't believe the Queen has declared war recently, has she? Maybe I missed it of course, I have been out of the country. But I don't believe Russia can be officially described as the enemy yet, can she?" Webster smiled. "Besides, I haven't sold anyone or anything Major. I'm not doing this for anything as vulgar as money. You're as bad as old Fitz there, always assuming the basest motives for everyone."

Jones snorted. "You serve a higher purpose, I suppose?"

"As much as you do," Webster sneered back. "At least I have thought about my choices, rather than just doing as I was told, like a little boy playing soldiers."

The General cut in. "Much as I hate to interrupt this touching reunion. There are other matters to attend to."

Gorev turned to Baburin, indicating the captives. "Comrade Commander, prepare yourself for a trip to Moscow. You will accompany the saboteurs on their journey south."

"Yes Comrade General."

Gorev went on. "You will travel in style, gentlemen. We shall arrange for one of our airships to take you, rather than the train. Much faster that way. In Moscow you will properly enjoy the, ah, hospitality of the Cheka. You will discover how Russia deals with spies and –"

"General?" Webster's interruption contained a note of urgency and they all turned to look at him. He stood at the bench of captured equipment, but now held one of the packs in his hand.

"What is it now?" said Gorev. "Take whatever you want. I have more important things to deal with."

"No General, you misunderstand. Commander Baburin, the explosion at the telegraph office – how big was it?"

Damn it, thought Jones. He had hoped for a little longer.

The Cheka officer looked confused. "How big? Big enough to destroy the building and kill seven of my men. Is that big enough?"

Webster frowned. "No Comrade. Not big enough by half." He looked back to the General. "When we dropped from the airship we were carrying four packs between us. Packs stuffed with dynamite charges and timing fuses." He hefted the bag. "This one, and the other, are almost empty. And if the explosives were not destroyed at the rail yard..."

Gorev seemed to understand at once. He stormed over to Jones and hoisted him up by the lapels, bringing them face to face. "What have you done with the other charges?"

"I don't know what you're talking about."

The General dropped him back into his seat and struck him across the face, the backhanded slap echoing round the chamber.

"Where are the rest of the explosives?" he shouted.

Jones worked his jaw before answering. "You'll find out soon enough."

This cool response tipped Gorev over the edge. His face turned crimson and twisted into an animal grimace. He pulled his pistol from its holster and shoved the barrel into Jones' face, pushing the Englishman's head back, grinding the weapon against his cheekbone.

"Where are they?" Gorev screamed, veins standing out in his neck and spittle flying.

Jones stared into the Russian's bulging eyes. "Go ahead," he grunted around the pain of the pressure on his cheek, "shoot me."

Gorev appeared to give the invitation serious consideration, pressing the pistol hard against Jones' face, fingers flexing on the grip. Abruptly he withdrew the gun and turned away.

"No Major Jones," his said, his voice quieter now, but infinitely more dangerous. "Not yet. But someone else shall pay for your lack of co-operation."

The General moved round the table and raised the pistol again, pressing the weapon against the back of Fitzgerald's skull. He looked down at the man seated in front of him and then back to Jones.

"Once more, where are the explosives?"

Fitzgerald looked up, his face bruised and battered, shoulders hunched beneath Gorev's menacing bulk. Jones made to speak but the other man gave an almost imperceptible shake of his head. Jones felt a hot flush of shame that he had ever doubted the loyalty or bravery of this man.

Webster stepped forward. “I doubt the Major will talk. He’s too wedded to his damned duty.” He shrugged. “We English can be pig-headed like that I’m afraid.”

Gorev returned Jones’ implacable stare for a moment before speaking. “I believe you may be right Comrade. But I cannot have the Major here thinking me a man of idle threats.”

The shot was incredibly loud, causing them all to jump in shock. A gout of blood sprayed across the table in front of Fitzgerald. His upper half slumped forward, his head impacting wetly on the table top, thankfully concealing his ruined face from view. The ringing of the shot faded away into stunned silence.

Eyes fixed on the still form of his compatriot, Jones spoke through gritted teeth. “I will kill you for that General. If it’s the last thing I do, I will kill you. I swear it.”

Gorev holstered his pistol. “Words Major. That is all you have. Words. And yet you refuse to say the words which could save your comrades...”

Moving to stand behind Maria’s chair, the General placed his hand on her shoulder. She visibly shuddered at his touch, although her gaze never shifted from the dead man across the table. The doctor’s obvious fear seemed to please Gorev, and he began rubbing a lock of her hair between his fingers.

“Perhaps Comrade Webster is right and your sense of duty will keep you silent, but I wonder if you also suffer from a misplaced sense of chivalry. Shall we find out?”

Balling his fist in her hair, Gorev pulled the woman from her seat, ignoring her father's protests. He pinned her against one of the room's support pillars, shifting his hand to cover her mouth before stretching out his other, palm up, toward the guard.

"Your knife, Comrade," he said.

Given the weapon, he raised the blade towards Maria's face. She squirmed, her eyes wide above the iron grip of Gorev's hand. She grasped his arm to try and prise it away, but the General was too strong for her. The Professor rose, attempting to go to his daughter's aid, but the guard stepped forward, swinging the butt of his carbine into the old man's side. Eisenstein collapsed back into his chair.

Ignoring the Professor's agonised moans, Gorev tilted the knife left and right before the terrified woman's face, catching the pale green light from the refinery on the blade.

"The explosives Major. Or the doctor becomes a Cyclops, like my friend Comrade Baburin."

*

Kowalski could scarcely believe this was happening. First Fitzgerald and now Maria. He stared over the table at Jones. The Englishman's face remained impassive. He'd clearly let them all die if it meant stopping the Reds in their tracks. Someone had to say something.

"Wait. Leave the Doc out of this."

The General turned his head. "You have something you wish to say?"

Kowalski chewed his lip, eyes flicking between Jones, the slumped mess of Fitzgerald, and the helpless woman.

Webster, still pale after Fitzgerald's sudden execution, spoke up. "General, let me deal with this. I have a feeling the Captain might be more reasonable than my stubborn compatriot."

Gorev nodded. "Go ahead Comrade, but my patience grows short."

"There's quite a difference between these two men. Major Jones here, he's a patriot, misguided but loyal. He's like a dog that cannot see the faults of his master. He does as he is told. He would never consciously betray his superiors."

The English traitor turned away from Jones and clapped his hand down on Kowalski's shoulder. "But this one? He's a different beast altogether. A soldier of fortune – he owes no loyalty except to the highest bidder."

Baburin was outraged. "You're suggesting we pay this saboteur? An enemy of the people? Ridiculous."

Webster waved the Cheka commander to silence. "Sometimes one should adopt the methods of one's adversaries. What do you say Captain? Do you still believe in capitalism? Could we come to some arrangement?"

Kowalski looked up at Jones over the table, holding the other's gaze for only a moment before his eyes slid guiltily away. Jones glared, hands balling into fists. "Kowalski..." he growled in warning.

"Now now Major," said Webster, clearly enjoying himself. "Leave the Captain to make his own decisions. All in the spirit of free enterprise, eh?"

Kowalski raised his hands, displaying the rope round his wrists. "Hardly free. More like blackmail." He paused, not daring to catch Jones' eye again. "But I don't want to end up like poor old Fitz. Go on, I'm listening."

"You Judas," spat Jones. "Is this what it comes down to?

Every man for himself?"

Kowalski hung his head, unwilling to respond. Webster however, was only too happy to speak. "But that's what capitalism always comes down to Major. That's why the system will always fail in the end. That's why—"

"Enough politics," snapped Gorev. "The explosives..."

"Ah yes. Quite right." Webster turned back to Kowalski. "Well Captain, here is the deal, as I think you colonials put it. Help us, and we'll let you live. Who knows? We might even let you leave. Simply show us where you and Jones planted your little bombs."

Kowalski raised his head, holding Jones' baleful stare as he spoke. "Him? He didn't place any of the charges himself. Typical officer – left me to get my hands dirty whilst he had a smoke."

Kowalski saw the spark of realisation in Jones' eyes as he spoke the lie. Thank God, finally the man gets it. He went on, injecting a note of bitterness into his voice. "The Imperials ain't paying me nearly enough to die for them. I'll show you where the damned explosives are."

Webster smiled in triumph. "See Comrade Baburin. Sometimes capitalism does have its uses."

The General released his grip on Maria and pushed the woman back into her seat. "You should thank the American. His mercenary nature has saved your pretty face, for the moment."

But Maria was clearly in no mood to be grateful to a turncoat, staring at him with undiluted revulsion. Ouch, thought Kowalski, if looks could kill, he'd be six feet under at least.

Gorev went on. "Baburin, take this man and recover the

explosives. If you think he is lying at any point, feel free to encourage him as you see fit." He thumbed the edge of the knife. "The removal of a finger or two can provide a great deal of motivation."

The Cheka commander pulled Kowalski from his chair and bundled him towards the door, a pistol pressed into his back.

*

Baburin marched Kowalski down the corridor toward the elevators. The soldier on guard snapped to attention when the Cheka officer spoke. "Come with me. We are to escort this prisoner to the surface. If he makes any attempt to escape, shoot him."

The guard shifted his carbine to point it at the captive. Kowalski could feel its aim as an itch between his shoulder blades as they stood waiting for the elevator.

"I'm going to need these free," he said, raising his bound hands in front of him. "Unless you want to defuse the charges yourself. Tricky business, fiddling with explosives. Ain't sure I'd want to try it with one eye..."

Baburin glowered at Kowalski, but nodded to the soldier. "Cut him free," he said, covering the captive with his pistol as the guard drew his knife and sliced through the ropes.

Kowalski rubbed his wrists as the elevator cage arrived, fingers tingling as his circulation returned. The guard opened the gate, moving to the back corner of the lift, carbine at the ready for any sign of trouble. Baburin took the other corner and Kowalski stood between them, sliding the concertina gate shut at the Cheka officer's instruction.

"Take us up," ordered Baburin and the guard turned the

lever on the control console. The cage shuddered and began its ascent.

"The first of the charges ain't on the surface," said Kowalski over the metallic jangle of the elevator's progress.

"Where is it then?" demanded Baburin.

Kowalski raised a finger. "Up there. On the cage roof."

Both men looked up and Kowalski seized his chance. He swung his arms up and out, the edges of his hands chopping into the exposed throats of the Russians. He felt the crunch of cartlidge as his right hand connected with the neck of the guard. Gasping for breath through a crushed larynx, the soldier collapsed. The strike with the left hand was less successful however, hitting Baburin on the side of his neck rather than full in the throat. The blow stunned the Cheka officer momentarily and threw him back into the side of the cage, but left him very much alive.

The gun in his hand came round and Kowalski grabbed for it, throwing himself at the Russian. The pistol fired, the bullet tugging at Kowalski's sleeve as it flew wide, the noise of the shot reverberating through the girders of the elevator shaft and reflecting back from the rock walls. With both hands clamped on the Russian's wrist, Kowalski battered the other man's arm against the metal railing. With a grunt of pain, Baburin opened his hand and the gun fell, clattering once on the floor before bouncing between the bars of the cage and disappearing into the darkness.

The Russian responded to the loss of his pistol by grasping his assailant's shoulders and swinging his head forward with savage force. Staggering back from the blow in agony, eyes streaming with tears and blood pouring from his nose, Kowalski stumbled over the dead guard and dropped to his knees. He shook his head stupidly, trying to regain his senses.

The Cheka man was on him before he could recover, hands locking around his throat. Kowalski flailed, clawing weakly at the Russian as his vision began darkening around the edges. He slumped lower as Baburin bore down, determined to choke the life from him, pushing him backwards onto the body of the soldier.

As the Russian loomed above him, face spattered with blood, his single eye burning madly, Kowalski's scrabbling hand closed around the hilt of the knife in the dead guard's belt. With his last reserves of strength, he pulled the blade free and slashed it across the other man's thigh.

The constricting hands at his throat were withdrawn as Baburin roared with pain, clutching at his leg. Kowalski sucked in a huge lungful of air and boosted himself to his feet. He took a step forward and swung his hand round in a wide arc. The strike was clumsy but carried the weight of desperation, smashing aside the upraised arm and plunging the knife to the hilt in the Russian's neck. The Cheka commander swayed on his feet, gave a single bloody cough, and then keeled over.

Numbly, Kowalski reached for the control lever, stopping the cage's progress. Suspended between levels in the twilight gloom of the elevator shaft, he sank to the floor beside the two dead Russians, taking in painful, grateful breaths.

*

Gorev used the telephone to summon two soldiers to remove Fitzgerald's corpse. The occupants of the chamber watched in silence as the men lifted the body and hauled it out, the dead man's heels dragging across the concrete floor. The blood spatter across the table remained, an ugly testament to what had occurred.

"You have accomplished nothing Major," said the General once the body was removed. He gestured to the observation windows, to the workers in their protective clothing, now filing out of the refinery. "Another shift finished. Another load of ore purified. Another step completed in our development of the most powerful weapon the world has ever seen." In the green light cast from the windows, the General's smile looked almost demonic. "It is a slow process, but it cannot be stopped."

"And once you have it?"

"Then Russia cannot be stopped either. For too long the other powers have looked down their noses at us, thinking us the backward child of Europe. No longer." He clenched his fist and stared down at Jones. "With this power, and the will to wield it, we will take our rightful place."

In Gorev's gleaming eyes, Jones saw the truth. "You mean *you* will take your rightful place, don't you? This is not about Russia at all..."

The General's tone grew more strident. "And why should I not be rewarded for helping my country? The people of Russia crave a strong hand, Major. That is why they suffered under the Tsars for so long. That is why they flocked to the red flag of Vladimir Ilyich in the Revolution – not because they were true believers in Communism, simply because the Romanovs had become weak."

As he finished this speech, Gorev seemed to realise he had said too much, revealing too much of his personal ambition before the guard and Webster. "Of course," he went on in a more reasonable voice, "All I want is to serve the Party for the glory of Mother Russia, in whatever capacity my country calls upon me to fill."

"How very noble of you."

"No less noble than your vain quest to stop us, eh Major? It is a shame your hired hand proved somewhat unreliable."

Jones bit his tongue, holding back the response he so dearly wanted to throw in the General's face. He had no idea what Kowalski had planned, but out of here, on the move, he surely stood a better chance of making an escape attempt. And if not, well at least he wouldn't be helping the Soviets find the explosives.

Very shortly, the charges would be going off and work at Kovdor would come to an abrupt, explosive halt. He could live with that. Not that he would of course, unless they could get the hell out of here in the next hour.

He turned away from Gorev's gaze, somehow nervous the other man might be able to read his mind. His eyes fixed on the bloody stain on the opposite side of the table, unable to stop himself from tracking the pattern across the wood.

"Just think," said the General, noting the direction of Jones' stare, "If you had been willing to co-operate in the first place, your companion would still be alive."

Jones was thinking of little else, but he'd be damned if he would let his guilt and shame be a source of amusement for the Russian. He glared back at Gorev.

"We both know that's nonsense. We're all dead men regardless. You and Webster may have convinced

Kowalski otherwise, but I know we're all Moscow-bound."

"Don't worry Major, any unpleasantness you suffer in the capital will be short-lived." He turned to Professor Eisenstein and his daughter. "Unlike the unpleasantness which you two will experience here."

The old man lifted his eyes to Gorev, his arm curled protectively round Maria's shoulders. "I beg you. Do with me as you will. But please —"

"Please what?" interrupted the General with a cruel laugh. "Please don't hurt your daughter?" He snorted. "Don't be naive, Professor. Don't you see? I *have* to hurt your daughter."

Eisenstein crumpled. "I'm sorry..." he whispered to Maria.

Maria took her father's face between her hands and stared at him. "No," she said, "don't give him the satisfaction."

Gorev seemed amused by the display. "What did you expect Professor? You are a traitor to your country and a personal embarrassment to me. And yet you remain too valuable to our efforts here for me to simply kill you." He narrowed his eyes. "With your wife no longer with us, I will turn my attention to the remainder of your family to keep you motivated. And to punish you for your contact with the Imperialists –"

This unpleasant conversation was interrupted by a sharp tapping from the other side of the room. All the occupants looked round to see a lone figure standing on the other side of the thick green glass of the observation windows. He was clad in a protective suit of heavy canvas and rubber, his face obscured by the metal bell of his helmet. He was tapping repeatedly on the glass with his gloved hand.

Turning away from his captives, the General stalked toward the window. “What is this idiot doing?” He looked at the guard who shrugged in response.

The figure was waving now, gesturing wildly, repeatedly pointing at the floor in an exaggerated fashion. Gorev stood before the glass, staring at the gesticulating man, anger beginning to take over from curiosity. “Go and see what the fool wants,” he snarled at the guard.

As the soldier moved towards the door, Webster turned away from the scene beyond the window and caught Jones mouthing instructions at the Professor and Maria, gesturing with his head. Struck with sudden realisation, the traitor shouted a warning to the General.

Gorev turned at the noise, frowning as first Jones and then the Eisensteins tipped their chairs to the floor. Before anyone could react further the chamber was filled with sudden light and heat and the locomotive roar of an explosion.

The heavy bulkhead door of the chamber blew inward, torn from its hinges by the blast on the other side. Propelled by a ball of flame, it tumbled end over end, sparks rising where it struck the floor. The guard had an instant to spot the approaching chunk of steel, enough time for him to realise what was happening, but not enough to even raise his hands. The door hurtled into his body, smashing him aside before crashing to a halt against the wall.

Around the ruined doorway, the walls were cracked and scorched. Ruptured piping, blackened and twisted, spewed clouds of steam. Scattered clumps of burning wreckage were strewn across the chamber, creating a thick atmosphere of acrid smoke. As the echoes of the blast faded, they were replaced with the piercing howl of the emergency klaxon.

Jones fought his way clumsily to his knees amidst the remnants of his broken chair, struggling to push himself up with his bound hands. He shook his head in an attempt to clear it, but the movement made his vision swim in and out of focus. Of Webster, and Maria and her father, he could see nothing through the smoke, but he spotted Gorev slumped against the observation windows, thrown there by the blast. The Russian had a deep cut across his forehead, and blood streamed down his face. As Jones watched, Gorev moved his head groggily, and struggled to rise.

With a grunt of effort, the General hauled himself to his feet. Leaning against the window, he turned his head slowly, bleary eyes tracking across the room and filling with fury at the sight of the kneeling Englishman. He began slowly limping forward, staggering first one way and then the other, fumbling for his holstered weapon.

The General stumbled closer, evil intent written plainly across his bloodied face. Jones found it impossible to force his own legs into action. The Russian finally managed to haul his pistol from its holster and raised it, struggling to hold it steady. Jones tipped himself forward and crawled, scrabbling at the ground as the weapon fired. The shot was wild, flying over the Englishman's head, Gorev unable to hold his aim.

Jones' hand closed around the leather strap of the dead guard's carbine and he hauled the gun toward himself. Lying on the floor, he raised the weapon clumsily in his bound hands. Squinting along the barrel at the blurred shape of his advancing adversary, he pulled the trigger.

Bullets spat from the carbine's swaying barrel, the recoil playing havoc with Jones' aim. Despite the wayward spray of fire, two of the scattered shots found their mark. The first caught Gorev in the chest, thumping him back a step and causing him to look down stupidly at the blood spreading across the front of his uniform. He brought his frowning face up in time for another bullet to take him beneath the chin, exiting up and out through the back of his skull in a spray of blood and bone.

The General dropped like a felled tree, his muscular frame crashing to the floor.

Part Three

Still clad in the protective clothing of a refinery worker, but minus the brass helmet, Kowalski barged his way into the observation chamber through the twisted remnants of the doorway. He stepped over the broken body of the guard, to where Maria and the Professor were helping Jones to his feet. Although they were dazed and perhaps a little scorched in places, he was relieved to find they all seemed at least half alive. Unlike the General, he thought, looking at Gorev's body lying full-length on the floor, a puddle of blood spreading out from the back of the skull.

"Good shooting Major. Sorry I couldn't be of more immediate assistance, but I definitely had a ringside seat," he gestured towards the window.

"Oh, I think you did more than enough Captain." Jones shook his head, his ears still ringing. "Are you quite sure you used enough explosives?"

"I didn't really have the time to tailor things. I liberated one of the charges from the Professor's laboratory."

As Jones' head slowly cleared he took in the state of Kowalski's face – crusted blood below a crooked nose, dark circles of bruising beginning to form around his eyes.

"Good grief. What happened to you?"

"Don't you worry none. You should see the other guy."

Maria moved towards Kowalski, wincing with sympathy at his injuries and laying her hand on his arm. "Captain, I owe you an apology. I should never have doubted you."

Kowalski grinned. "Well perhaps you'll allow me to escort you to dinner once we get out of here. Surely that's the least you could do?"

The doctor arched an eyebrow and was about to respond when Jones interrupted. "Let's concentrate on the getting out of here part before we start arranging our social calendars. Where is Webster?"

The Professor pointed to a prone figure on the other side of the room. "Your spy has taken a nasty knock to the head. But he is alive. I think."

"We'll soon see about that," growled Kowalski.

"Hold up there Captain," said Jones, "I want him alive. We're taking him back to London with us."

Kowalski couldn't believe what he was hearing. "You've got to be kidding me Major. We've already got two people to worry about on the way back, and now you want to take prisoners?"

Jones nodded as he began gathering up their packs of equipment. "That's exactly what I want. Webster comes home so he can tell us how much information he's given to the Bolshies. And we want the names of his contacts in England."

He went on, talking over Kowalski's objections. "There's no time to argue, go and wake him up. I'm surprised that damned siren hasn't summoned half the soldiers in Siberia by now."

Kowalski smiled, distracted from the issue of Webster. "Heh. I'm sure they're on their way Major, but they'll be a little while yet. You know those other charges we placed in the laboratory?"

Jones turned to look at him. "Yes? What about them?"

"I sent one of them upstairs."

*

Three levels above, Sergeant Volikov shouted to be heard over the wail of the klaxon, trying to generate some kind of order from the chaos at the head of the elevator shaft.

He had been a hundred feet up the tunnel, halfway to the exit, suffering little more than a sprinkling of dust from the ceiling when the blast had shaken the rocks around him. Unlike these poor bastards, he thought, spotting a hand poking out from beneath the rubble.

The bright flash and roar of the explosion had been followed by the rumble and crash of falling machinery. Seeing a group of men go down beneath the tumbling metalwork of the elevator gear, Volikov had offered up a most un-Communist prayer of thanks to God he hadn't been caught in the carnage. Gathering men as he went, he ran back down the tunnel and took charge of the scene in the absence of any more senior officers.

"You!" he bellowed at one of the soldiers. "Stop gawping and get those bodies out of there." He grabbed another man. "Fetch some engineers, and some bloody crowbars or something." He pointed at the twisted girders and scorched wood blocking access to the shaft. "We need to get all that shit cleared out of the way. Understand?"

The soldier nodded dumbly before turning and running up the tunnel. Volikov shook his head at the stunned faces of the younger men around him. Bloody children. This was nothing compared with a real battlefield. He raised his voice again, shoving confused soldiers this way and that, sparing no curses and delivering kicks and thumps here and there to get them moving. He figured a few blows and some harsh language would be nothing compared with what the

General would do to them all if he ended up stuck down that damned hole for too long.

*

Jones and Kowalski stood before the cage doors of the elevator station, peering up into the dark. Clangs and crashes and muffled shouts echoed downward, accompanied by the occasional tumbling girder or splintered plank of wood. The beams of the elevator shafts themselves were twisted out of shape, and whole sections of the wooden stairway which spiralled round the cavern walls had been swept away by the impact of debris from above. Jones doubted they would be receiving any visitors any time soon.

"Good work Captain. Although it does rather beg the question of how on earth we're going to get out of here."

Kowalski looked crestfallen. "Sorry Major. It seemed a swell idea at the time."

"I'm sure it did."

"Maybe there's a back stair?" suggested Kowalski weakly.

"A tradesman's entrance, eh? If so, you'd have thought we'd be knee-deep in angry Bolshies by now. I don't recall seeing any on Hanson's plans, but let's check with the Professor and the good Doctor."

They returned to the observation chamber where the two scientists stood watch over a groggy Webster. Eisenstein and his daughter were silent as Jones explained the situation, and both shook their heads gravely when asked about other stairs.

"There is only one way in or out of the complex," said the Professor. "It was designed that way. For security."

Webster chipped in, a sickly smile playing across his pale face. "So you're trapped here after all Major? It's only a matter of time until the soldiers get through, and then this little caper of yours will be over."

Jones turned a hard gaze on the traitor. "Oh do be quiet Webster. Yes, it is only a matter of time, but not in the way you think." He reached into his pocket to check his fob watch. "If we don't find a way out of here in the next hour or so, then it really will all be over – soldiers or no." He gestured towards the tall windows. "The mine, the refinery, the whole kit and caboodle, is going to end up in quite a mess. You do remember how much explosive we brought with us, don't you?"

Webster swallowed nervously and didn't reply. Well, thought Jones, the situation had not improved, but at least he'd wiped the smile off that bastard's face. Now Webster looked as worried as the rest of them.

The rest of them that is, except for Professor Eisenstein, whose face was suddenly lit up with new-found hope. "The refinery!" he exclaimed. "That's it!"

They all stared at him.

"The ore for the refinery. It comes in on a conveyor belt..."

Maria picked up on her father's excitement. "Which leads directly from the mine shaft..." She turned to the others. "Which has a ladder to the surface!"

*

Made clumsy by the heavy canvas and rubber of the protective suits they now wore, the five of them made their way across the refinery floor. Jones had been initially surprised the view through the thick glass of his helmet was not cast in shades of green, but the peculiar colour had been the result of the tinted observation windows rather than any particular lighting within the factory itself. However, whilst his sight was as usual, his other senses were all dulled within the cocoon of the suit.

He could hear little inside the helmet beyond his own breathing and the faint hiss from the compression flask on his back. The air it supplied had a metallic taste and a rubber smell, a most unpleasant combination. But much better than the alternative, he supposed.

Webster turned and cast a sullen look back at him. Jones waved him forward with his pistol. The turncoat had initially refused to don the suit, or enter the refinery, loudly protesting that he would not be taken back to England to face the hangman's noose. Jones had made it abundantly clear that the traitor's choice was a bullet now, or a chance to convince Buckingham to let him live later.

For a moment Jones had thought the other man might choose the bullet, to die there and then, a Hero of the People. But he watched as Webster's last dregs of courage slipped away in the face of the harsh reality of the pistol's muzzle. Clearly there was little point in choosing the romantic ideal of becoming a martyr to the revolution if there wasn't anyone there to witness the act.

Now, hustled forward, Webster scrambled up to join the others atop the broad plates of the conveyor system. Kowalski covered the prisoner as Jones climbed up in turn. Getting to his feet, Jones waved them on and the group headed along the belt towards the dark tunnel from which it emerged.

Ducking down and crawling inward, Maria took the

lead, followed by her father, moving stiffly under the twin burdens of protective clothing and age. Then came Kowalski, glancing back regularly to check on Webster. Jones brought up the rear, keeping his weapon trained on the traitor's back as best he could as he crawled forwards.

They activated the small electric lamps attached to their headgear and crawled on though the cramped space, helmets and air flasks bumping and scraping along the low ceiling of the tunnel. Clouds of dust were stirred up by their passage, swirling like golden snow in the beams of their lamps. Deadly stuff though, Jones reminded himself, no matter how pretty it looked.

After five minutes of crawling and bumping their way through the darkness, the walls and ceilings abruptly opened out and they blinked in a dim light. They clambered down from the conveyor belt to find themselves on a thin ledge, about three feet wide, which ran round the circular walls of the mineshaft. This was obviously where the massive drill engine paused during its daily return to the surface, depositing its cargo of uranium ore scoured from the depths of the earth.

Checking Kowalski had Webster covered, Jones shuffled forwards to peer over the edge. The weak light from above allowed him to see the walls continue down perhaps twenty feet before all was swallowed by inky blackness.

"How deep?" he shouted to Maria. His voice boomed incredibly loud inside his helmet, but he knew Maria would barely be able to hear him through her own headgear.

"A thousand feet," she yelled back, "Straight down."

The doctor grabbed Jones' arm and pointed with her

gloved hand. There, fixed into the cold rock of the wall, were the first rungs of a metal ladder, rising up the sixty or seventy feet towards the pale circle of daylight which marked the surface.

*

In Kowalski's head the climb up the ladder was taking forever. The Professor above him was struggling to match Maria's pace up the rungs, stopping regularly to catch his breath and forcing Kowalski to wait beneath. This might be the last such halt though. Tipping his head back, he saw Maria disappear over the lip of the mine at the top of the ladder, only fifteen feet or so above where the Professor rested.

Kowalski leaned back further and the enormous drill unit suspended above the mineshaft came into view through the glass of his helmet. Its concentric rings of cruel teeth descended to a sharp point seemingly aimed straight down at the insignificant figures clambering up the side of the mineshaft. He thought of the explosive charges strapped to the machine's supporting pylons. The timers were ticking away up there, and they couldn't hang around for long, no matter how tired the old man was. When those charges blew, the drill unit would collapse, plugging the mine shaft permanently. And spectacularly. Kowalski wanted to see the results of his demolition efforts, but preferably from a distance.

He lifted his hand, ready to tap the Professor on the ankle to encourage him onwards, but the elderly scientist began to haul himself up once more. Kowalski gave a grunt of respect. Fair play to the old man, he was holding up pretty well, all things considered.

Before he restarted his own ascent, Kowalski looked down to check on Jones and Webster. The gaping void below did its best to make him vomit. As before in the elevator, the enclosed space and yawning depth filled him with a cold dread. He was careful to keep his gaze fixed on the men on the ladder beneath rather than letting it stray further out and down towards the beckoning blackness.

The two Englishmen were twenty feet below him on the rungs, about halfway up from the conveyor belt ledge. They were making poor time, even worse than the Professor. Webster wasn't in great shape, remembered Kowalski, he'd struggled badly on their trek from the airship drop. And Jones wouldn't want to get too close to the traitor's feet. It would be hard enough trying to keep Webster covered with the pistol, essentially climbing one-handed. You wouldn't want to stray within kicking distance of a man with nothing to lose. Kowalski still thought it crazy bringing the prisoner along, but he figured Jones was the boss and it was his call.

He turned back to his climb. The slow pace frustrated him once again, but finally he watched Eisenstein clamber over the top. Reinvigorated at the prospect of getting out of the mine and out of his helmet, Kowalski practically scampered up the last few rungs before crawling out onto the snowy ground and flopping onto his back. He stared gratefully up at the sky. Although grey cloud filled his vision and the sun was nowhere to be seen, he thought it looked damned-near perfect. Much better than being stuck down a hole.

He pulled himself to his feet and took a quick look around. Other than Maria and her father, nothing moved within the area enclosed by the rail tracks. The steam-shovels and tractors were still, their drivers no doubt pulled away to deal with the trouble in the complex. Over by the tunnel entrance, men could be seen scurrying back and forth as black smoke curled out between the doors. It gave him a nice warm feeling to see it.

Webster appeared at the shaft's rim and Kowalski watched as the traitor struggled away from the top of the ladder, hunched over, obviously gasping for breath. As Webster wheezed, Jones' helmet popped up over the edge.

The sudden noise of an explosion made Kowalski turn. Even muffled to a hollow crump by his helmet, the sound was unmistakeable. A cloud of smoke billowed up into the sky and a tongue of flame bloomed within one of the clusters of piping. The first of their Russian timers had finished its ticking. Kowalski and the two scientists stood transfixed as a huge round boiler, weakened by the blast, ripped itself apart in a spectacular burst of steam and flying metal.

*

Webster straightened up to see the others all facing away, distracted by the explosions. If he wanted to avoid the noose, this was his chance. His only chance. He charged towards Jones, still on hands and knees, moving off the ladder. Looking down, his vision limited by the brass helmet, Jones was oblivious to Webster's approach.

With a fierce, desperate glee Webster stamped his booted foot down on Jones' gun hand, feeling bones crack even through his heavy sole. Jones reared back in agony, the pistol dropping from his shattered grasp. He tumbled onto his side, unable to do anything but clutch at his injured hand.

With the helpless man lying before him, Webster gritted his teeth and channelled all his rage and fear into his kick. The blow caught Jones in the ribs and knocked him backwards towards the mineshaft. Clawing at the earth with his good hand, Jones slipped over the edge.

Webster looked down into the shaft, expecting to watch his adversary plummeting into the dark. Instead, he saw Jones, fist locked around the top rung of the ladder, hanging above oblivion. Legs flailing, scrabbling for purchase, Jones' hold was precarious, but for the moment at least he was very much alive. The man had the lives of a cat, seethed Webster. Still, he could afford to leave him for a few seconds yet. It was time for the mercenary to receive his comeuppance.

When Kowalski turned back from the blasts, Webster was already raising Jones' pistol. The Floridian must have realised Webster had the upper hand, but he went for his carbine all the same. Brave, thought Webster, but stupid.

He pulled the trigger and relished the sight of Kowalski going down hard. He watched as the doctor dropped to her knees beside the fallen man, her anguished cry audible even through his helmet. Cry all you like dearie, he thought. You and your father will not be far behind.

But first Jones. Webster stepped to the top of the ladder. The man still hung below, arm twisted, helmet and air flask bashing on the rock as he tried to swing himself round onto the rungs. Webster grinned to himself as he moved his foot over the hand clutching the ladder. Why waste good ammunition? Time to break those other fingers.

The bullet thumped into his shoulder and spun him around. He dropped his pistol and clutched at the wound.

He reeled, feeling faint as the shock of the impact was replaced with the beginnings of a dreadful pain. He looked up to see the woman, still kneeling beside Kowalski, holding her pistol in two hands.

Webster lifted his hand to ward off the shot he knew was coming. When it did, it smacked wetly into his chest, lifting him up off his feet and throwing him backwards into the abyss. He plunged silently into the dark, the pale circle of sky dwindling above him as an ice-cold numbness spread through his body.

*

Over the waves of agony from his crushed fingers, Jones could feel his other hand beginning to lose its grip. He swung his injured arm across himself again, trying to turn and get his feet to the rungs, but the pain of the attempted movement foiled him once more. That bastard Webster might well have sailed past him a moment ago, but Jones knew he would shortly follow.

It seemed unfair somehow for it to end like this. A bullet he could have taken, indeed he'd invited one from Gorev earlier. To be shot by the enemy, to fall in combat, that was how he'd always expected it would turn out. But falling down a hole? That was just damned embarrassing.

He felt a hand grasp his arm through the thick fabric of his suit, easing the strain on his shrieking muscles. His unseen saviour began to pull at him, not enough to lift him out, but enough that he finally got turned and managed to place his feet on the ladder.

Summoning his last reserves of strength, Jones pushed upwards with his legs. Another hand grabbed at the back of his belt, and hauled from above, he slowly, painfully, clambered out of the shaft to collapse on the ground.

God, but the earth beneath him felt good.

*

Lights danced behind Kowalski's eyelids. A female voice calling his name filtered down through the noise reverberating in his head. Slowly his scattered thoughts gathered themselves and he willed his eyes to open. The light set off fireworks of pain in his skull and he let out a groan.

Maria gasped and pulled Kowalski to her. He struggled to make sense of what was going on, but when he finally realised, he returned the embrace. Every cloud, he thought, winking up at Jones over her shoulder. The Englishman gave an exasperated shake of his head.

Kowalski looked round. He was propped up against the wheel of one the enormous steam-shovels which sat idle amongst the slag heaps. The others must have carried him here from the top of the shaft. Or, more accurately, Maria and her father must have carried him. Jones looked about done in, wincing as the Professor wrapped a strip of fabric around his hand.

"What the hell happened?"

"I got my bloody fingers broken. You managed to get yourself shot." With his free hand, Jones lifted up the Kowalski's helmet. There was a large dent in the brass, the deformed slug of a bullet at its centre.

"That explains the noise." Kowalski shook his head, ears still ringing. "I thought someone had smacked me with a bell. Where's Webster?"

"He got on the wrong side of the Doctor here. She sent him packing." Jones gestured back towards the mineshaft.

"Much as I wanted to return him to England, I have to admit I'm glad to see the back of him."

Kowalski untangled himself from Maria and held her so he could see her face. "Are you alright?" he asked.

She stared back at him, a mix of guilt and pride in her face. Kowalski looked in her eyes and saw it all – the conviction that she had done the right thing conflicting with the hot shame that came from killing for the first time.

"Don't worry. You did good Doc. Way I see it, you saved the hangman a length of rope."

Another explosion ripped through more of the track-side machinery, off to their left this time. They all looked up as the ball of flame curled skyward.

Jones finished tying off his makeshift bandage. "Up you get Captain. We have a train to catch."

"A train? You said we had an airship coming?"

The Englishman shook his head. "Captain, Captain. Surely you don't believe every story you hear over a drink?"

*

Jones climbed up onto the locomotive's footplate. The engineer stood with his back to him, looking out at the chaotic scenes around the tunnel mouth. Soldiers staggered from the tunnel coughing from the smoke, and groups of men unwound fire hoses before donning clumsy breathing apparatus that reminded Jones of their recently abandoned factory suits. Thus clad, the group of fire fighters hauled their equipment toward the entrance. Clearly all was not well within the complex.

Another blast erupted nearby, blowing apart some sort of pumping station. The engineer jumped at the sudden noise, and then cringed at the clatter of debris falling on the roof of his cab. He jumped even higher when Jones tapped him on the shoulder.

"Apologies my friend," said Jones. "I did not mean to startle you."

"Comrade Major, you scared the shit out of me." The man waved at the carnage. "What the hell is going on?"

"German saboteurs, Comrade. They are blowing everything up. We need to move your train so they don't get it as well."

The engineer threw his cigarette butt out into the snow and tugged his hat down.

"Right. Let's get the old girl warmed up."

He tapped at a couple of gauges and nodded to himself. He pulled at one lever, and tightened a valve, then turned to Jones.

"Won't take long. She just needs stoked up. Don't suppose you'd give me a hand?"

Jones nodded and smiled. "No problem Comrade. But first, let's get the cars disconnected..."

He jumped down from the footplate, keeping the train between him and any eyes on the tunnel side. The engineer leaned out of the cab and shouted after him.

"Don't you want to move the cars too?"

Jones ignored the question and beckoned the man to join him. The railwayman looked confused but climbed down and followed Jones past the coal tender. There the two of them withdrew the heavy pin which attached the locomotive to the rest of the train.

"I still don't see why we couldn't move it all," said the engineer as they marched back.

Jones turned, his pistol raised. “Because we only need your locomotive.” He shrugged. “Sorry Comrade.”

Kowalski and the two scientists materialised from their hiding place behind one of the nearby wooden sheds. Jones indicated the terrified engineer.

“Captain, I was just explaining to our friend here about the German saboteurs.” He gave Kowalski a wink. “Perhaps you could keep an eye on him whilst I get the engine ready to depart?”

“Jahwohl,” deadpanned Kowalski in a truly terrible German accent. He pulled the carbine from his shoulder and turned it toward the unfortunate railwayman.

“Hande hoch!” he ordered. “Bitte?” he added uncertainly.

Jones winced at Kowalski’s pronunciation and climbed aboard the locomotive. He checked the firebox and threw two shovelfuls of coal inside. He looked at the pressure gauge. Good. As far as he could tell, they were ready to depart. He turned and waved the two scientists aboard and then signalled to Kowalski.

The Floridian nodded and raised his weapon, peering down the barrel at the helpless prisoner. “Run!” he barked.

The engineer needed no further encouragement, bolting off into the heart of the mine workings. He sprinted and ducked left and right, without looking back, desperate to avoid the hail of bullets which he clearly expected to come after him. No bullets flew though. Kowalski was climbing aboard the locomotive almost as soon as the man had started running.

Jones handed the shovel to Kowalski and moved to the controls. Kowalski looked unimpressed.

“Now I reckon this is what Webster would have called an inequitable distribution of labour.”

Jones shrugged. “Perhaps. But it seems that whilst anyone can shovel, only one of us knows how to drive this thing.”

Kowalski dropped his pack with a grunt and moved into position between the coal tender and the firebox, shovel at the ready.

“Get us moving Major.”

Jones opened the throttle, releasing steam pressure into the pistons. The locomotive slowly moved forward. As further explosions ripped through the buildings around the mine, the train’s departure went unnoticed. Its speed steadily increasing, the engine climbed the gradient around the side of the depression, giving its four passengers a grandstand view of the unfolding chaos below. A number of fires now blazed, thick black smoke mingling with the billows of escaping steam from hundreds of broken pipes and ruined boilers.

Then, with a flash, the first of the charges under the central drill unit detonated. With a metallic groan, audible even over the rest of the destruction, one of the tall pylons supporting the massive cylinder began to buckle. The huge mechanical monster started slowly listing to one side, the remaining supports bending and cracking under the enormous pressure of its unstable weight.

When the second charge exploded, the damaged structure could take no more. Another of the support struts snapped and the drill unit itself came crashing down, its jagged rings of metallic teeth flying apart as the steel cylinder shed its skin of plating and pipework. The roar of its collapse echoed round the bowl of the mine, and the shriek of the steam pressure escaping from its shattered innards was like the death wail of some dreadful creature from prehistory.

The guards at the gate had no idea what was going on. They had been standing watching as the entire mine facility appeared to blow itself apart in a frenzy of steam and fire, when surging out of the clouds of smoke, the black apparition of the locomotive rumbled up the tracks. Before any of them could react, the vicious snowplough blade on the engine's front broke through the thick chains securing the gates and smashed them aside.

Clear of the mine at last, Jones looked back. He shared a fierce smile of satisfaction with Kowalski as they surveyed the destruction in their wake. Now all they had to do was get out of Russia.

*

The Captain atop the walker looked down on his men as they arrayed themselves around the rail yard. The telegraph message from Kovdor had been garbled, but there seemed to have been some sort of accident and then someone, somehow, had managed to steal the damned mine train.

Probably some poor bastards the Cheka had hauled out there to scrabble in the dirt, he supposed. Most likely couldn't take it any longer, took advantage of the confusion, killed their guards, and hijacked the train. He couldn't really blame them – the mine was a shit-hole. But orders were orders, and his were to round up the escapees. If they were lucky, they'd get sent back out to the mine again. If they were unlucky, well, the next thing they'd be digging would be their graves.

From his vantage point up in the walker's hatch, he was the first to spot the locomotive as it crested the hill on the outskirts of the town. Ducking his head down he ordered the pilot to move. From his cramped seat within the cab the man nodded, adjusting his goggles and turning back to his controls and the narrow viewport. With a crunching of gears the walker lumbered forward, positioning itself astride the railway tracks.

The Captain shouted down to his men below and they lined up on either side of the rails, ready to surround the engine. Satisfied with the men's deployment, he looked up to the approaching locomotive once again.

He frowned. The black engine was much closer than he had expected, almost into the yard already. Now the walker was still, he could suddenly hear the roar and rumble of the locomotive's approach. With the noise came the sick realisation of how quickly the oncoming train was travelling. He yelled down into the cab.

"Get us off the tracks! Now!"

The walker jolted into motion once more, the pilot hauling desperately at the drive levers. The Captain peered out of the hatch and watched the thundering approach of the engine in horrified fascination. The walker lifted a clumsy foot. Too slow, thought the officer. Too slow.

The locomotive sped between the ranks of soldiers, some too shocked to react, some quick enough to raise their weapons and snap off useless shots at the impervious engine. The snowplough blade caught the walker below the knees of its metal legs, slicing clean through the first and twisting the other beneath it. The steel box of the walker's body was tipped up and lifted into the air before the round black frontplate of the train's boiler smashed into it. Despite the heavy armour, the frame of the cab crumpled, crushing the pilot to a pulp and pinning the Captain's legs between twisted plating. With his top half hanging helplessly out of the hatch, the officer began to scream as the engine ploughed on, the wreckage of the walker carried along, impaled on its front.

Belching smoke and steam, shedding chunks of debris, the train roared through the engine shed, smashing aside the buffers which marked the end of the line. Off the rails now, the locomotive thumped and bounced on the uneven ground. With a screech of tortured metal, it tipped over onto its side, but still it slid on, ploughing up a jagged trench in the frozen earth.

Finally, with an almighty crunch, the runaway train struck the high brick wall of a warehouse at the yard's edge. There, fifty feet beyond the end of the line, it came to rest, spent, the ruin of the walker and the front half of its boiler embedded in the building. After the cacophony of the crash, relative silence fell, broken only by the tumbling of displaced bricks and the hiss of steam leaking from the engine's fatal wounds.

The soldiers ran towards the wreckage through the engine shed, following the path of destruction. Arriving at the train's final resting place they stood stunned, mouths hanging open as they took in the carnage. As they began looking at one another in shock, the explosives detonated.

Jones and Kowalski's last two bundles of dynamite contained enough force to convert the locomotive's footplate and cab into shards of metallic shrapnel, propelled outward by an expanding ball of flame. This deadly hail cut a bloody swathe through the squad of soldiers. The handful of men who survived the first blast were dropped by a second, larger wave of explosions as the munitions piled in the warehouse began to go up.

Stacked shells for Soviet artillery, huge round bombs designed to be dropped from airships, and box after box of bullets and hand grenades – all of them exploding, one after another, in a massive chain reaction of fire and noise.

*

Two miles back down the tracks, Kowalski and the others paused in their trudge through the snow and lifted their heads as the sound of the huge blasts rolled out.

He turned a quizzical look on Jones. "We didn't put that much explosive on the train. You reckon someone started a war without letting us know?"

They looked east, watching as an enormous fireball ballooned up into the sky above the trees which masked their view of the town.

"Whatever it is, it should prove an excellent diversion," said Jones. "Come on, the river cannot be far now."

They slogged on through the snow, their march accompanied by the regular beat of explosions and the rapid tattoo of exploding machine gun ammunition. They reached the river without seeing a soul, and turning east, they followed the turbulent grey waters towards the town.

Murmansk was in chaos. Panicked officers and factory foremen yelled conflicting instructions at groups of men. Thick oily smoke surged upwards from the direction of the rail yards, the sure sign of a major fire taking hold. Alarm bells and klaxons added to the general din and confusion, punctuated by the occasional booming reports of more shells going off.

They slipped through the pandemonium on the streets unchallenged. Dodging between the rushing squads of men and the great rumbling tractors, they worked their way steadily along the waterfront, heading for the docks. Once beneath the forest of cranes, they walked the edge of the wharf, Jones eyeing up the smaller boats moored between the cargo ships.

Kowalski leaned close. “Planning a boat trip Major?”

“Something like that.”

“I have to warn you, I get real seasick.”

“Don’t worry Captain. I doubt we’ll be out there long enough for you to need your sea legs.” He stopped and looked down on a small steam launch. “This will do. And no crew about to repel our little boarding party.”

Jones clambered down the slippery steps and hopped aboard the small vessel, disappearing into the wheelhouse. The others followed and Kowalski helped first Maria and then her father traverse the gap between steps and boat.

Jones poked his head out from the cabin. “Let’s get her running. Shouldn’t take long. Captain, be a good chap and prime the kerosene...” He indicated a rusted pump handle at the stern, then turned to the Russian scientists. “Take a seat. With any luck we’ll be on our way in no time.”

As Eisenstein and his daughter slumped gratefully onto the bench at the side of the deck, Kowalski moved aft. If it wasn’t shovelling coal, it was pumping kerosene, he grumbled to himself, yanking the fuel pump up and down. The mechanism screeched in protest and his muscles echoed the complaint. This had been the longest day of his life, and he now found himself aching in places he hadn’t even realised *were* places.

"Good show Captain," shouted Jones from the wheelhouse after a couple of minutes. "That should do it."

Kowalski stopped pumping and leaned heavily on the handle. As he recovered his breath, an indignant voice echoed down from the wharf above.

"Hey. What the hell are you doing?"

He looked upwards to see the furious bearded face of a Russian sailor. He could have been nothing else, clad as he was in a donkey jacket, waterproof galoshes, and a woollen hat. The seaman stood at the top of the stone steps, a large wooden box held in his hands.

Kowalski smiled up at the irate seaman. "Relax Comrade. We're just borrowing it for a little trip. We'll bring it back safely."

"The hell you will." The sailor's face darkened further and he looked around. "Bloody Army. Think you can do anything you damn well please. I'll find someone to sort this out..."

Damn. Time to finish this, thought Kowalski. He whipped his carbine round off his shoulder and raised it towards the figure above.

"Down you come Comrade. Quietly now."

The sailor's eyes went wide, but rather than complying with Kowalski's instruction, he threw his crate down at the gunman in the stern of his boat. Ducking the tumbling box which smashed off the deck beside him, Kowalski brought his gun up again, but the sailor was gone, out of sight beyond the edge of the wharf above. Out of sight, but Kowalski could hear him just fine, loudly shouting the alarm.

"Major!" yelled Kowalski. "We need to go. Right now."

To Jones' credit he didn't ask why, but immediately threw the launch's throttle fully open and jumped to the forward rope, knife in hand. Pulling his own blade from his belt, Kowalski cut through the aft cable. As Jones returned to the helm, the vessel slowly puttered away from its mooring.

Kowalski went to the door of the wheelhouse. "Jesus Major, doesn't this thing go any faster?"

"No, sadly. I don't think it does. Why the sudden departure?"

Kowalski gestured back towards the wharf where a group of onlookers clustered. The boat's angry owner shoved his way to the front of the crowd, tugging at the sleeve of a Red Army officer. The soldier peered across the widening gap between launch and dock. Kowalski snapped off a salute, willing to try anything to buy them a little more time. The baffled soldier gave a half-hearted salute in response, clearly struggling to make sense out of the enraged sailor ranting at his side.

Shouting and gesturing toward the stolen boat, the seaman continued his tirade, and eventually the message got through. Abruptly the officer began shouting himself and raised his pistol to take aim at the boat, now fifty feet away.

"Get down," shouted Kowalski, and they all crouched as low as they could.

The shot's flat crack echoed over the water, the bullet smacking into the wooden lintel of the wheelhouse doorway.

"Be glad he doesn't have a carbine," said Jones.

"He doesn't. But I think his friends might..."

The officer was now flanked on the quay by a dozen men, all swinging their weapons up to their shoulders. Kowalski lifted his own and pulled the trigger. The onlookers on the quay scattered at the harsh clatter of the gun, civilians and dockworkers diving for cover. The soldiers stood their ground though, and bullets flew in both directions across the water. Facing twelve carbines, Kowalski was seriously outgunned and was quickly forced to duck down as the enemy shots started thumping into the boat.

The windows in the wheelhouse shattered, adding flying glass to the storm of splinters which engulfed them. Maria and her father lay prone on the damp planks in the bottom of the launch, sprayed with debris but out of the direct line of fire. Kowalski prostrated himself beside the wheelhouse, occasionally holding his carbine above his head and haphazardly firing in the general direction of the shore. A shard of glass struck his forehead and he felt his face and hands peppered with splinters, but somehow no bullets found their mark.

The relentless fusillade from the shore poured bullets into the wheelhouse. Jones stayed crouched within as the projectiles ploughed through the flimsy structure. He kept his head down, but reached his hands up to the controls, one pushed forward on the throttle lever, the bandaged one loosely holding the helm, keeping the launch fixed to a vaguely straight course away from the quay.

Kowalski had had about enough, of the day, of the country, and most of all, of being shot at. He raised the carbine again and sprayed fire blindly towards the quay, finger locked on the trigger.

"Stop. Shooting. At. Me." he shouted over the barking of the guns.

With a click, his carbine fell silent, its circular magazine empty.

"God damn it!" he yelled in frustration, throwing the useless weapon over the side. Why did the other guys never run dry? He hunkered down, hands over his head.

Slowly but surely, the boat pulled away and the hail of fire gradually diminished. Eventually, when they were about two hundred yards out into the Kola Sound, the firing stopped altogether.

Kowalski pulled himself to his feet and made to check on the others. After finding Maria and her father were shaken but unhurt, Kowalski moved to the wheelhouse. He found Jones standing, eyes wide, poking his finger through one of the holes in planking. The walls were riddled with them.

"Are you alright Major?"

Jones blinked and looked down at himself, absently brushing broken glass and fragments of wood from his clothing. "Yes..." he said. "I think I am."

Kowalski glanced back to the dock where uniformed figures continued to point at the escaping vessel. "Figure it won't take long for them to get a boat out after us. And it ain't likely to be any slower than this one, is it?"

Jones tore his glazed eyes from the holes in the planks. He gave a shake of his head and seemed to come back to his senses. "Quite possibly. But I rather hope our little boating trip is almost over."

"I don't see any of your dreadnoughts out here Major. If

you've got any other tricks up your sleeve, this would be a swell time to play them."

Jones looked over Kowalski's shoulder and gave a tired smile. He clapped the Floridian's arm reassuringly.

"Cheer up Captain. Here's our ride..."

*

Anderson rubbed at his unshaven face with both hands and massaged his aching eyes. He had been watching Murmansk's waterfront through the glass of his periscope since first light. They had arrived the previous night and taken advantage of the darkness to spend some time on the surface replenishing their air flasks. But now *Nautica* was back where she belonged, lurking invisibly twenty feet below the gentle swell, half a mile offshore, well away from the obvious routes in and out of port.

He had spotted the black smoke curling into the sky from the other side of the town and wondered if it had anything to do with his mission. Whatever was going on, it had caused a sudden flurry of activity throughout the parts of Murmansk he could see. Made nervous by all the movement ashore, he called his crew to action stations, although to give them their due, they couldn't have been any more alert. Four days submerged in an untested vessel, penetrating a foreign country's waters certainly served to keep the men on their toes.

"Hold on," he said to himself. "What's this?"

He clicked the handle round on the periscope. Atop the retractable steel pipe which poked above the waves twenty feet above him, the lens head smoothly substituted one set of optics for another, changing the view reflected in the mirror from a panoramic to a closer, magnified image.

Anderson refocused and turned the periscope, tracking the view in on the small boat now pulling away from the shore. He winced as he watched the soldiers on the wharf open up with their weapons. Although the magnification was not powerful enough for him to properly see what was happening aboard the craft, and of course he couldn't hear the shots, he dreaded to imagine the pounding the crew of the launch were taking.

"I believe our passengers may be arriving shortly," he announced to the bridge crew. "Prepare to take us up."

He watched as the little boat slowly pulled out of range of the gunners on the shore. Time for *Nautica* to make an appearance. He slapped the handles of the periscope up into their recesses and let the mechanism slide smoothly down.

"Blow the tanks. Take us up. Half ahead."

The ballast tanks were immediately pumped dry with air from the compression flasks, increasing the submersible's buoyancy. As her screw began to turn and push her forward, the steering fins were angled and her bow lifted. Anderson adjusted his footing as the deck sloped.

Nautica broke the surface in a boiling spray a dozen yards in front of the steam launch. Streams of water ran off her back and a welcome if weak sunlight flooded through the glass dome of the bridge. Looking up, the Captain realised this was the first time his vessel had ever surfaced in daylight.

"Mister Dixon," he said into the speaking tube, "please assist our passengers aboard."

*

The launch bobbed in the water alongside the submersible, tiny in comparison. Dixon's men threw lines with grappling hooks and hauled in the little boat, securing it to the larger vessel. Dixon stepped forward and tossed down a rope ladder to ease the climb up the curve of *Nautica*'s hull.

The occupants of the boat pulled themselves up the ladder and Dixon got his first look at their passengers. The old man and the woman looked about done in, and sympathy for their condition overtook his initial shock at seeing a female come aboard. He instructed his sailors to get them below and turned to the next arrivals.

If he'd thought the first couple looked exhausted, well, he didn't know what to call these two. Their faces were drawn and haggard beneath the cuts, bruises and dried blood. They leaned on each other as they reached the deck, looking like nothing so much as a couple of bilge-rat drunks who had been on the wrong end of a particularly vicious beating.

But as they approached, Dixon revised his opinion. He reckoned that it was the Bolshies who had found themselves on the wrong end of things. Despite their bedraggled appearance, there was something dangerous about these men, a look in their eyes which suggested they were not to be trifled with. They had a hardness about them, the sort of men he'd want on his side in any kind of a fight. Dixon snapped to attention and offered a salute.

"Welcome aboard, gents. Captain Anderson is waiting on the bridge."

The two men nodded wearily and limped towards the hatch. As the first man descended the stairs to the companionway below, the other looked up towards the shore and the town.

"I shan't be sorry to see the back of this place."

"No sir. Looks a little cold for me sir."

The man turned his eyes on Dixon and gave a smile. "Oh, it got plenty hot enough..."

Dixon followed him down the steps, securing the hatch before making his way along the cramped corridor towards the bridge. Their four guests stood, wrapped in blankets, looking round at the controls and the glass dome overhead.

"Everything secure topside?" asked his skipper.

"Aye sir. Hatches shut."

Anderson called out orders. "Flood the tanks. Make our depth thirty feet."

"Aye aye sir," chorused the crewmen stationed around the bridge.

The passengers watched nervously as the water crept up the glass above their heads until it washed right over the top. The weak daylight filtering from above faded as they slipped down into the depths.

Anderson stepped forward, hand thrust out in welcome. "Welcome aboard the *Nautica*. Major Jones I presume?"

Jones introduced his companions in a round of handshakes. The old man began asking excited questions in his broken English, clearly fascinated by the submersible and curious about its operation. The skipper laughed.

"Relax Professor. We have four days sailing ahead of us. Plenty of time to show you round and explain how everything works." He paused, struck by a thought. "That is, if I'm allowed to tell you anything. I'll take your guidance on that Major."

Jones looked at the two scientists. "I would say you could tell them anything they want to know Captain.

Professor Eisenstein and his daughter have given up everything to help us against the Communists. They may be Russian, but they are without a doubt, some of the Empire's bravest friends."

Anderson nodded gravely and looked at his Russian passengers with new-found respect. "Very well, I will see Mister Dixon here gives them both a guided tour as soon as they've been fed and got some rest."

The skipper spotted Dixon's look. "Problem Chief?"

Dixon felt his face flush. "It's only... begging your pardon, sir. But, well, it's frightful bad luck, sir. Having a woman aboard."

"Good grief man. What would you suggest? We cannot exactly put her back ashore now, can we?"

"I'd like to see anyone try," laughed Kowalski. "The Doc here don't take kindly to being told what to do". He slipped his arm round the woman's shoulders. "Besides, this little lady has been a regular good luck charm for me since I first met her."

The doctor rolled her eyes, but Dixon noticed she made no attempt to shrug off the arm.

Jones snorted. "What a load of old tosh. You've almost been killed umpteen times in the last few hours."

"Heh. Exactly Major. Almost been killed. *Almost.*"

Captain Anderson smiled with the others before turning to the man at the helm. "Set course for home. Full steam ahead."

Sitting in his office overlooking Lubyanka Square, Comrade Director Felix Dzerzhinsky of the Committee for State Security reached again for the closely-typed pages of the report. Scowling, he flicked through it once more. His most reliable investigators had been despatched to Murmansk to unravel the events of two weeks before, but even they seemed unable to verify the important details. That the mine at Kovdor had been targeted by saboteurs was beyond doubt, but what these mysterious men were said to have accomplished seemed beyond belief.

How could a handful of agents possibly have destroyed the entire facility? Not to mention wiping out half of the arsenal of the Red Army in the North? And had these sinister figures really assassinated so many high-ranking officers and scientists, along with the local head of the Cheka itself?

Dzerzhinsky's brain whirled with questions, none of which were satisfied by the report in his hands. And putting his own questions aside, he knew Vladimir Ilyich was livid, demanding an answer to the most pressing question of them all: who had dared launch this attack against Soviet Russia's most secret project?

At least there Dzerzhinsky felt he could provide the Comrade Chairman with an answer. He had one report of the infiltrators speaking German, but more importantly there were dozens of witnesses who swore they had seen the escaping spies picked up by a submersible. One of the Kaiser's damned u-boats – prowling within Russian territorial waters. Outrageous.

What had possessed the Germans to commit such an open act of aggression? He had always had Bismarck pegged as a more wily and subtle opponent than this clumsy move suggested. Well, regardless of the reasons, the Kaiser and his Iron Chancellor had made a mistake this time. And with Europe on the brink of war, and Lenin spitting blood in his rage, this mistake might very well prove fatal

***

Acknowledgements

I hope that if you got this far, you enjoyed reading *Red Mercury.* Writing a book is something I had wanted to do for 25 years. Actually finishing one and being able to share the story with other people is a hugely satisfying feeling. Hearing what readers think is another. If you did enjoy it, or have any comments, please let me know on my blog at redmercurysteampunk.blogspot.co.uk

Thanks to everyone who read any of my many drafts. Your comments and encouragement undoubtedly made the story better and punchier at every turn and kept me going at it even when my enthusiasm had waned. Particular thanks go to Doug, Richard and Alex for being my beta readers.

A special tip 'o the hat to my wife Alison (the scariest editor ever), for putting up with months of me disappearing every evening to tap away on the laptop. And thanks also to Danny and Blythe, for making me a very proud dad.

2139531R00078

Printed in Great Britain
by Amazon.co.uk, Ltd.,
Marston Gate.